Catherin Hope's "V" Chronicles

Pandora's Box

C.B. Mantooth

authorHOUSE®

AuthorHouse™
1663 Liberty Drive
Bloomington, IN 47403
www.authorhouse.com
Phone: 1-800-839-8640

First published by AuthorHouse 7/7/2011

ISBN: 978-1-4567-5139-5 (e)
ISBN: 978-1-4567-5140-1 (hc)
ISBN: 978-1-4567-5141-8 (sc)

Library of Congress Control Number: 2011907404

Printed in the United States of America

CHAPTER 1

I HAD BEEN HERE IN Biloxi for its own small eternity. I needed a way to earn money and make myself known. A longtime friend of mine gave me an idea on how to earn money from humans. He introduced me to Anthony. He now is my business partner of our club-strip club that is. Tony and I did well for the establishment we decided to open. I put up the money and he gave his name. Well you see I am a vampire. And a real live-well dead descendant of Pandora. I know what you're thinking I'm going to tell you about her box but sorry to displease you the only thing I know or have about her box is my club. I named my strip club Pandora's Box.

My club and a pinkish tint in it there was track lighting all lined in my club. The biggest stage was a long rectangle about 9 feet. At the end of the rectangle there was a square a pole was lined in the middle of it. There were chairs that lined the stage. The dancer got on the stage by a stairs at both ends toward the wall. There was a door on the wall behind the stage-that went to the ladies dressing room and our offices. Anthony and my office was the same size. They were next to each other passed the three other offices.We had two managers, besides me and my co-owner Anthony; Dean and Bobby, there good kids. There are three bars in my club, one right to the left when you entered-that bar also had a mini stage next to it. There was one in the middle of the club further into the establishment. Behind that middle bar was the DJ booth the last bar was in the high roller section. Pretty basic

1

lay out if you ask me. There was a ramp leading to the high roller section and even had its own host.

It was Saturday night, we just closed and I got change back into my business suit. I went out to the front of the stage and got the dance books out. Waiting for all the girls to come out and pay their rent. Rent for the weekends were 250 dollars. What can I say I wasn't greedy? By the way, rent is what you charge dancers to work at your club. They are all private contractors and you either charge them by the dance or rent. I charge them rent. With over 50 girls you just couldn't get greedy. Wendy a woman that I hung out with on my free time was buzzed on the money she made tonight. She was constantly chit chatting-I don't mind her pointless banter but the other girls seemed to be getting a little annoyed. I've known her for 5 years now. She in an odd way was a friend, maybe even a best friend.

You didn't come across to many of them. Being the undead was troubling enough, with title of Strip Club owner to Vampire-to Vampire hunter. I've been in Biloxi for its own small eternity. I've owned the club for the last 10. When Katrina hit, I was real reluctant to rebuild, but when I found out that the Hard Rock Casino was going to give another build after the storm I thought why the hell not.

My job as the club owner was always fun. I loved the club-I loved the girls. I always told them to go to school and make something of their dreams, but to be honest with you a lot of them don't. I'm not knocking on the girls who do though, touché to them.

Wendy would be joining me for after work entertainment. I'm sure she would be bringing home some party favors, I never ask these days. She always surprises me, in a good way. She doesn't ever do or say anything that would make me uncomfortable, but then again what really could with someone as old as me?

I would like to see my friend go to college but knew well enough that she didn't have the self-esteem it took to go off to school. I for seen her getting a job at the casinos later in life, when she was too old to dance. Unless I didn't turn her, which I did think about every now and then, she never led on that is what she wanted. I think that's why I so fond of her.

After I got home I got situated. Wendy always came in and went directly to her room to change. I'd have given her a room because she was over so much. My house was pretty big with 6 bedroom's 4 bath roomsand one level. The floor was tile. I had some oriental rugs laid out in the high traffic areas like the living room and dining room. The bedrooms were carpeted. You'd come up to my house from a gravel road to a paved half circle drive way. Then you were met by two red French doors. My house was cream stucco, with tons of plant life.

You'd walk in to a big foyer and to the left there was a door, which led to a hall that went into the kitchen. There was a wall on the right with a giant mirror. Also a table to place my shoulder holster and keys, I know what you're saying why a vampire would need a gun-well as much as you can run and fight another of your kind it's always easier to kill them with the help of something. Ripping out hearts could get a little messy sometimes; scratch that-all the time.

The hall to the right from the door had all the bedrooms down them. My bedroom was the last door in the hall. Wendy's room was the first on the left. Her room had a bath room in it and the room next to her had one too. The rooms on the right side of the hall shared a bathroom. Why does this all matter-well I'm trying to set the mood-chill out.

My living room or pallor was straight ahead. There was a fire place and a television mounted to the wall on the right. I had my collections of books on the far back of the wall. I had a lot of seating in my living area of browns with very vibrate pillows of reds and oranges. I guess it was my yearning to see the sun. I had a big back yard with a jacuzzi. Wendy seemed to love the back yard. It had a bed back there that was covered by anawning. I had a lot of flowers and plant life in the back yard as well. Wendy came out from here room in a skirt that was a sweat pant material and a tank top with a little plastic baggie in her hand.

"Check these out-I got these new pills from Mike the valet. He said they came from Miami. But I seriously doubt that. They're called pure gold. They're pretty yellow-probably really smacky." She held one up. I took it and popped in my mouth.

"Does it taste gross?" I made an ugly face and she started laughing. She got herself one out.

I was in the kitchen getting me something to eat. I was also in search of my cigarettes. I have to remember to pick some up next time I went to the store-also to get gas. There was something extremely wrong with a little woman pushing a big monster truck into a gas station. People would stare-well I guess it's not like they don't stare anyway.

"If you were hungry you should have let me know-I am always willing to offer my wrist for you." She smiled to me and I smiled back.

"How many girls were on tonight?" She asked quietly.

"There were 52 girls tonight. What do you think of the new girls?" I asked her. She walked to the microwave and brought out my bottle.

"Bottle or glass?" she said.

"Bottle is fine." She handed it to me with the cap loosened.

"Tracy that's the younger of the two, she's 18 and I don't think she'd ever seen a pair of stiletto's in her life. She's got a pimp so she's super jack up. I hate the way she talks and she gives us a bad name you should fire her." She said with kind of an attitude. But she was letting me take in what she said.

I don't really get involved with my dancers lives. It's kind of a fluke I ended up Wendy's friend. This guy was giving her shit at the Black jack table while I was walking by, if he wouldn't have had spilt anything on me I don't think I ever would have said anything. I guess it was her lucky day. I recognized her immediately-she was one of my best girls. She's hard not to notice and remember.

"On the other hand Bailey is a pro. You don't have to worry

about her she's making tons of cash already. Thanks a lot boss just more competition for me." She said it kind of laughing I looked up at her and she stuck her tongue out.

Wendy had nothing to worry about, she was about 5'8 which made her about amazon height with heels, had long red hair that was past her enhanced double-d breast. High cheek bones and thin nose thicker lips. Her eyes were a chestnut brown. She wore contacts every now and then to make them blue. I thought she was attractive in a slutty sort of playboy fashion.

Wendy was telling me about what the girls were bitching about and I wasn't completely paying attention. I just liked her company because she filled the silence with noise, and she wasn't afraid of being alone with me. Good girl. I finished my blood and placed it down. I didn't know if I should bring this up to my friend but what the heck.

"I felt his presence again tonight." I said it softly. I didn't really want to admit this. I had been in somewhat of a predicament. I always had this nagging feeling that someone was watching me and stalking me to some sense, which is annoying because I'm the one who hunts the vampires in town. His presence was strong-actually to be completely honest he's presences was the strongest I've ever felt-ever.I knew if he kept fucking with me I'd be out there to track him down. He would be easy to find too-with as strong as he allows himself to be felt. But then again he could be doing it all on purpose-pallor trick per se`. Hard to tell though vampires these days are way different than my day.

"Really, you seemed to be on guard tonight but I didn't even put two and two together. Hmmm, he's an old one huh." I never said he was old."I wonder if he's hot." Boy Wendy was always one for vanity and money. She was a normal woman of these days if you ask me, unless you found a 24year old mom, priorities change. "You know what I mean Catherin? Usually the really old ones are old looking and withered and ugly. If he's been bugging you I would think he'd be hot. Since you're like a bronze goddess." She was teasing me. How did this little human woman get so comfortable to tease me? It made me a little happy she felt that comfortable with me. She's a no non-sense kind of woman and I liked that about her. She doesn't let anyone give her shit. Good for her.

"It's hard to say, he's never looked into a mirror while close to me. I know he's staring at the club. He's never gets close to the door." I gritted my teeth a little. I was intrigued none the less but it bugged the fuck out of me. I wanted to know this mystery man.

After an hour I started to feel the effects of my ecstasy pill. I opened my arms up to Wendy and she made her way over and placed herself in the middle of my legs. She leaned in to kiss me. I kissed her back. She was a soft kisser. She wasn't the aggressive type-I know she's very submissive. She reached down and caressed my breast softly. I could feel inside my legs tense up and a hard little knot form. I grabbed her breast hard. Her breasts were fake and almost too big for her body. But she was still sexy naked. I pulled her shirt over her head and she lifted her arms to let me. I unclipped her bra and laid her back and started to suck on her nipples. She was running her fingers through my hair. I reached up her skirt and she didn't have any panties on. He sex was moist and she had a hard little knot between her legs as well. I pulled up her skirt so it lies around her waist and she sat up with her elbows. I spread her legs and started kissing her thighs. He legs was quivering a little. She was ticklish so I had to get to business. I laid my tongue on the little hard knot in her legs and she let out a loud moan. She fell to lay flat on the couch. I had her one leg up and I inserted two fingers in her and she let out another moan. I was lifting her with each of my thrust of my hand in and out of her wet sex.

"You have to stop don't go so fast or you'll make me cum." Wendy protested to me.

"And why would that be a bad thing." I whispered back to her. She threw her head back and continues her protest quietly. Within a minute she was shaking and I felt a river on my hands and in my mouth. She's lucky I didn't have neighbors or we'd have cops here all the time. She got to her sense and sat up. I was glad to have done something nice for her. Within a half an hour she was at it with me again. She smiled to me.

"Now it's your turn." She said to me softly. I just smiled to her and laid back.

CHAPTER 2

WHEN I GOT UP today there were messages on my answering machine-what time was it? As I played it back it was my partner Tony, he was pissed because some of the Council was at the club. Shit! I got up and did my normal routine-I skip the shower because it would have taken too long to get my hair dry. I got out a dark maroon suit. Black tights laced up into a black garter, black fitted body suit. The top fit very nice against my fuller D breast. All my suits are all sexy suits. I didn't own anything that didn't look appeasing to the eyes.

When I got to the club and entered I saw the Council members there. Vivian and Cal were leaned towards each other in deep conversation. Dmitri was there looking so perfect with his older style suit, all in black. Like a reckless cowboy. He seen me first, he stood up as I was walking towards the table. When Vivian saw me she rose as well, and Cal followed right after her.

"My apologies, I don't know what I was thinking with not remember such an important engagement." Trying to sound as humble and empathic as possible, to be completely honest with you I could care less for these vampires, which the Council there were 12-here in front of me there were only 3. Well Dmitri was fine. He always made advances to me but I never knew if it was for himself of for the Council. I can't deny that I would feel guilty for not taking him up on his advances.

"Apology accepted Catherin." Vivian said to me like a bitch. I really didn't like this woman but she was after all another employer to me.

"What brings you down to Biloxi?" I was only curious. There was really nothing down here in Tri Area South for the Council members unless they came down here to take more money from me, which they seemed to enjoy.

"Have you found any one on the list that we faxed you?" Vivian asked.

"You're speaking of the bounty list?" I asked back.

"Yes that's the one my dear." She snickered to me. I really wasn't this vampire's dear, I'd really like to have a boxing match with this woman maybe I'd gain a little more of her respect.

"The term of endearments is really not necessary." I relayed to her.

"Thank goodness, I hate having to play nice." She was smiling a little so at least I knew she finally was being truthful to herself.

"To be honest with you, I haven't looked it over really, but what I did look over, you still have the same people on the list. Are they are hard to kill, or did you leave these vampires for me to kill?" I asked back trying not to let her take away my hospitality. Vivian leaned in and started whispering into Cal's ear, all I could think is wow so fucking professional. As the thought was bypassing my head Dmitri leaned in,

"You look great Catherin, Do you hunt regularly?" Dmitri whispered to me. I had to smile, not the most promising thing to do as a vampire but I loved smiling. I also liked to make the act of breathing, yes we didn't have to but it felt so freaking good to me.

"I do, I go to De Soto Nation Forest all the time." I whispered back to him. Dmitri looked disgusted for a moment.

"The glow isn't from hunting in your city?" He asked still in shock a little.

"You know as well as I do hunting humans is against the law and if I'm not totally wrong it's enforced by the Council 110 percent." I looked to him and winked. He smiled he was coming around.

"I never realized you could hunt animals and get a glow like that your tan skin is brilliant?" Dmitri made his small protest to me. I was happy to lead Dmitri with a surprise. You don't surprise vampires much. I'm almost certain he's been feeding off people for so long that blood from anything else would seem a little strange to him. But blood is blood. The synthetic stuff all taste the same to me, but animal blood tasted like wild blood. It had its own unique taste. I wasn't even so sure if it was an enquired taste or not. Vivian and Cal had stopped with their little whisper session.

"When you get some time please try to track them. Also we come for your quarterly dues." She was opening up a big leather binder, then flipped opened a receipt book and looked up some numbers wrote it down quickly and handed it to me.

I personally wasn't very pleased with having to owe any more money to them. They didn't even reside in the Tri AreaSouth, (Mississippi, Louisiana & Arkansas) but they sure did make it hell to participate with the damn Council. Sometimes I wonder why I just didn't go rogue, I could take Vivian and her dear pet Cal, I wouldn't want to hurt anything as beautiful as Dmitri, but then again I didn't think he'd fight against me, probably with me. Day dreaming is not the best for vampires like I said. I took the receipt and stood up,

"I'll be right back, let me write you a check." I said.

"No, we'll take cash." Vivian said right away. I really was holding onto a string at that second I was so happy that Tony came up and squeezed my arm and flung me around. I walked away from the table with every ounce of me holding back the urge to jump on the woman.

"Catherin I'm so proud of you." Anthony said to me.

"You are? That's good at least one of us is." I answered back holding my urge to scream.

"How much is the ticket?"

"It 50k, I mean what if we didn't have the cash, would they take it in blood?" I was curious.

"Catherin we do have the cash, don't be ridicules'. This isn't the only I've invested in for us you know that." He was kind of laughing when he said it to me. I didn't have to think of it, Tony here made sure we made money-he's asked for 20k, and two weeks later his was depositing 100k into my bank account. How he did it I never asked but he knew how to make moneyand I love it.

"Give them the cash Tony I'm going to go and sneak out the back." I said trying to leave right as I said it.

"The hell if you are, you're taking this to them and you're sending them on their way, than whatever you want to do after you can do." Anthony scolded to me. I know he's just human and in some odd way I had respect for him.Also he could also bitch like any of the girls that worked for me so he could be a miserable person to be around. I just looked at him while he got one of the thick bags we have out from our clubs merchandise. After the money was all tucked away, and the feeling of pure utter defeat settled in, I walked my once money to its new owners.

"Here you go, do you want to count it?" I said gritting my teeth so I wouldn't sound bitchy. Vivian looked like she was high, so made me wonder how straight edge the Council was-really?

"No, you've never tried to cheat us, I'm sure it's all there." She said looking in a pocket mirror and puckering to it. I didn't know if it was so good to be that good with the Council. I was too annoyed to really put any of it together though.

"Please Catherin looked into tracking those vampires from the bounty." Cal said. That had been the first thing Cal had said to me all night.

These must be southern Vampires that like to gamble. Most vampires were forbidden on playing Black Jack and Poker at casinos. But a lot of casino's catered to them with vampire Black Jack dealers and Poker dealers, also with them only being allowed to play against each other.

"Yes of course." I was rushing them to the door now. I really couldn't care about them or their damn list. I wanted them out of my club with their comp blood and drinks. I was sick of them sucking money out of me because that is all they ever seem to do. As I ushered them out of the club Dmitri seemed less likely to leave. He pressed his hand against the swell on my back.

"What are you doing this evening?" Dmitri said softly. This made me think of the other times I've denied him my company;I have really denied him it for the longest of time; but always in the back of mind I thought the Council has apart in his actions.

"I have no plans I'm going home after you exit the club and I'm relaxing till the weekend." I smiled. I could always smile to Dmitri. In that moment I thought he should tread very lightly and of course he didn't.

"May I join your evening escapades?" He asked so sweetly.

"Do you feel it's necessary? I mean wouldn't the Council have an opinion about it?" I said.

"No, not of what I'd be aware of, the Council is very fond of you. You're as straight as they get and you're one hell of a business woman. Your vampire tracking is in professional standing-outstanding." He said that very calmly. If he only knew that my luck usually was unlucky with people on the bounty usually stalking out to track me.

He was kind of eyeing me. I really didn't think he cared about my vampire tracking though, not one little bit. Dmitri was tall-black hair maybe to his shoulders, he always kept it up in a ponytail against his head when I saw him, had blue eyes which contrasted really nicely with the darkness of his hair. You could tell when he in his former life he was a white man with a tan skin, he must have had the tan when he was turned because you saw the faintness of it now in the afterlife. He had a strong jaw line with a long nose and thin lips. I'll say it again he is very attractive if you like the wild western villain cowboy look. I thought about it for a second. I guess if I accepted his offer we could fly down to the National Forrest for a hunt. I haven't hunted with anyone in the longest time. This is also a chance to know the mysterious Dmitri my; my body shivered at the thought.

"Well it sounds interesting. What hotel are you staying in?" I asked.

"The Hard Rock, it's the one that has the best cocktails, even has the vampire bars." Dmitri relayed to me. And yes, they did seem to cater us quiet well.

"Do you have a car?"

"We have a driver." He moved his eyes to the front of the long covered walkway in front of my club. There was a white limo at the end.

"Ok, you'll just have to ride with me." I said as calmly as possible. I didn't want to seem too eager or excited. He beamed a smile-ouch-He was a sexy man.

"Allow me to tell my partners." He walked out to them and got close Vivian's ear, Cal didn't seem like he had much authority, but just because he was not the one doing all the talking didn't mean anything. Usually the bosses liked to have someone else blurt out orders, it would point any anti vampire protestors out trying to stake the wrong vampire. Vivian leaned in and told Cal, Cal and Vivian gave me an interested look. Than both in unison gave me a distinguished nod, all I could think was I'm in for a ride.

CHAPTER 3

W E DROVE IN SILENCE to my house. He would look out the window and back to me every so often. When I pulled onto my gravel road Dmitri seemed to tense up. I guess new city-gravel road-there was room for vampires to get nervous. I entered my house and took off my pumps and started to remove all the clutter from my body. I threw my jack on the table next to my front door and took off my holster. Put my keys down I started to walk into my house and I forgot about Dmitri.

"I'm so sorry, please come in." You do have to invite vampires into houses. You see how long it's been since I've had company of my kind.

"I was curious to see how long you'd let me stand out there before you notice I wasn't behind you." He said it so calm.

"Of course I know you would have shut the door you're nothing but a gentleman." I tried to be reassuring.

"I wouldn't go out and say all of that." He was giving me a devious smile. He was sexy that was for sure. And you can tell he lived off that attention as well.He was a ladies man-he emanated it with his persona.

"I have to make a phone call. I'll make us some martinis and blood will that be fine with you?" I asked

"That would be great, a martini sounds wonderful."He smiled to me and turned around to scan my books. I walked into the kitchen and got some blood from the fridge-popped them into the microwave. I flipped open my phone and called Wendy. She was off today and if she was thinking of coming over she'd be here at any moment. She answered on the 2nd ring.

"Hello?" Wendy said, almost screaming. It was really noisy in the background.

"Where are you?" I asked.

"I'm in Gulf Port at the Grand View. It's Sunday. It's bingo night." Yes it had slipped my mind that she liked her bingo.

"Yes, I remember. I have company tonight so I'm just letting you know." I quietly said to her.

"Really, who is it? Do I know them?" She started to get snotty.

"Yep, it's Dmitri."

"Get the fuck out of here! You're with Dmitri the Council member?" She was shocked and extremely excited.

"Ah huh, so I'll see you tomorrow."

"He's so freaking hot! I want to know everything!"

"Ok, until than be safe."

"I will mom." She started laughing. She was being a major snot head now so I hung up the phone. There's no need to say bye to encourage her on with her little rant. I took out the Vermouth from the freezer and poured the measured shots into the shaker. Gave it a shake, by than Dmitri walked up to the bar looking into the kitchen. I placed a martini glass in front of him and poured out the frozen goodness. I walked over the microwave and got the blood out. Gave that a shake and placed it in front of him as well.

I led him to the back yard-opening my French-doors and walked him out to the covered bed out in the middle of the yard. I lit sometiki-torches around the bed. Dmitri took a seat at the foot of the bed. I had a big wooden tray in the middle of the bed for drinks and stuff. He took lead and placed his drinks on it pushing the ashtray with his drinks.

"So what is it that you'd like to do tonight?" I asked.He was quiet, I'm sure he had an idea on what he wanted to do. I wasn't so sure if he'd pursue what I had on my mind on doing. That would be a nice change for me.

"Whatever you come up with is fine with me." He said calmly. I thought of a bunch of things, that all consisted without clothes. Even though I didn't know if it would be crossing any boundaries? I didn't want to go that far with a member of the Council. Did I? You know having them in your arsenal would always come in handy. Hmm possibilities were endless right now.

When we were there in silence he leaned into me. I watch him so carefully, he gave me an eye and made eyes noticeably looking me up and down, finally he stopped and pressed his hand against my lower back right where I had my cigarettes placed in between my skirt and my body suit, I had took off my jacket when we got into the house. He pulled them out. If I were a breather I would have been holding my breath, but instead I let out a nervous laugh. He was looking right into my eyes. Just pools of blue surrounded me. He leaned in and went to fetch my lighter that was pressed in-between my breast. His hands were firm taking the lighter. There was nothing in the way he took it that he felt he was being pushy or over baring. He winked at me as he lit his cigarette. Well I thought does he know me and my body so in definite that he knows where my cigarettes lay.

"Impressive Dmitri, you found those cigarettes all by yourself?" I got out almost in a choke.

"You help, the way you are sitting I could tell where they lay on your body, your very sexy body." I wasn't fishing for a compliment so I was just wondering what exactly did he want from me, the thought had crossed my mind a bunch of times that he just wish to seduce me and I'm just another game for the Council to play. I grabbed the cigarettes from off the bed and fetch one myself, lit it and inhaled. I was looking into Dmitri's face and as I reach to touch him he countered with touching my hand with his bringing our palms together.

Immediately I was swimming, I saw a man coming in and comforting him. He was southing him, Dmitri was hurt it seemed more emotionally pain than physical pain. I felt the comfort from the older man, and the comfort he was giving him, than I realize the older man wasn't a man at all, he was a vampire. It must be his maker. As I started to pull away we rushed back into the lighted tunnel and there was I. It was raining, I remember that night like it was yesterday. I opened a door to a man and his wolf dog. They had gotten stuck in the rain from traveling. It was so wrong for a woman my age not to have a husband back in my time in the ages. The man I saw was my maker. I pulled hard and just like that, I was on the bed again. I was a more than uncomfortable now.

"What is it do you think you'll accomplish by being here tonight Dmitri?" I scolded to him. He looked famished, but he manages to speak beyond it.

"I just want to know you. Is that wrong? Am I wrong to want to know you Catherin?" He spoke it to me so calmly. I can't deny-but it intrigued me a little.

But was it wrong for him to do that to me. What expense would it be for him and me just to have a nice silent night together like vampires can? I was happy to see my cigarette in the ashtray so I grabbed it and inhaled. If I was going to have an overnight visitor I might as well be comfortable.

"I want to trust you because I want to know you too-but I just don't know." I took a breath out. He was much more careful now, he touched the top of my shoulder and in a swift graceful motion's rubbed his hand down my arm. He let out breath and I didn't take Dmitri for a breather.

"I'm sorry, I don't know how good that will hold to gain your trust but that's all I'm coming up with. Tell me Catherin how long have we been coming to your club you can honestly say you've never wondered about me to?" He softly protested to me. The truth was-I was extremely curious. Every time they leave I would end up being hard on myself for not taking him up on his advances.

"I've always been curious about you Dmitri." I whispered to him. He stared at me lightly.

He started to smile a little. Leaned in and kissed me on the cheek. I don't think he leaned back all the way before I took my chances and sprung on him like a waiting cat stalking its prey. He kissed back with much conviction running his fingers through my hair. He guided me so I sat just inches in front of him. I pulled off his ponytail holder and his hair hung loose on his shoulders. I ran my fingers through it and pulled his head back. I kissed his neck than I bit him. He moaned loud into the sky. He had me swimming through time. I saw a lot of his past in a blink of an eye-it took me into a world unknown. But after my vision all that was left was the throbbing between my legs. He pushed off the tray on the bed and the drinks went flying. He eagerly pulled at my skirt he found where the zipper was and unzipped it. I started with his shirt. I was doing everything in my power not to rip it completely opened. He helped me by doing some buttons his self. Getting to our bare skin seemed like a task all in itself. When my skirt was across the yard and he was pulling down his pants I got to see him in the full nude. I couldn't help but smile. I was on my knees and trying to get my body suit over my head he came to me while it was over my face and he pulled my body so it pressed against his, his cock was hard and I could feel the heartbeat in it. He pulled the body suit over my head for me and then he ran his fingers through my hair he then pulled me down into the bed. He started to kiss my breasts. He was doing fast circles around the nipples and he pushed his shaft against the knot in my legs. He rubbed it down to my slit and took some of my wetness with him. He wanted to tease me I saw. I growled and flipped him over to get on top of him. I grabbed his cock and he let out a moan.

"Are we going to do this?" He asked me. I started to kiss him again. I sat above him and let his sex penetrate my sex. We let a moan out together. "I guess we are." He whispered back to me. I started to feel my heart rumble in my chest. He smiled a naughty smile at me and switched positions on me. He was on top of me gazing at me with his deep blue eyes. He was thrusting in and out of me wildly and he went down on my chest and bit me. I let out a semi scream. I wasn't use to anyone taking my blood. He sucked till I got dizzy. My blood would keep him high for a long time. "Turn over." He asked so nicely I wanted to start laughing. I scooted back and turned over. He rubbed his shaft up and down my slit and found where it was the warmest and wettest. He slid into me again bringing his body to lay on mine. He pumped so hard he lifted me with each of this thrust.

"I'm going to cum." I told him. He ran his fingers through my hair and pulled my head back. He was licking my cheek and neck. He started moaning loudly in my ear.

"We will have to climax together than Catherin." He said. He reached under me to and pushed against the knot in my legs and started to rub it vigorously. I started to feel hot and I could tell he felt it too. Before I could take another breath or even blink my eye I felt the climax take hold and run it's madness in me. I shivered against his hard strokes. He stayed in me still a pressed hard into my pelvic area for a small moment. Then he slid out of me and lay there on the bed.

I crawled off the bed and grabbed his hand. He came with me his manhood swinging with his steps. I brought him to my bed room and I laid him down. I sat there and realized I wanted a cigarette so I leaned over him to grab my smokes and he intercepted me. He grabbed two and went back for my lighter. I smiled as he handed me a smoke.

"Did that just happened?" I lazily protested.

"Yes it did." He said softly. He was looking down on me with a slight smile on his face. We would be connected now, my blood was thick I knew he would feel me for a long time-through his blood exchange he was feeling at peace; that was just great I thought.

"What's wrong?" he asked.

"I'm not sure it seems all too much like a dream." I didn't know what to think of any of it.

"I hope it's one that you don't want to wake from." He softly protested to me.

He nailed it, in that sweet moment I didn't want anything to change. But these things never work out to good. And how much of a relationship could I have with a vampire who lived across the country?

"Yes, let's not wake up." I said.

He sat up on my bed and put out his cigarette. He plucked my cigarette out of my hand and put it out too. He rolled over and got between my legs. His eyes glowed so bright. I felt trapped him his gaze. I smiled and he smiled back. He leaned in to kiss me again. I kissed back because he was here for my advantage. I felt his man hood stiffen again and he smiled that same devilish smile he always got. I leaned into his face to kiss his sweet lips again. I'll be honest with you I took advantage of my guest tonight-I so well deserved it.

CHAPTER 4

DMITRI STAYED TILL TUESDAY. Dmitri was from another Tri Area-Tri Area East Washington DC Virginia and Maryland. He owned his own bar called 'Drop Pitt' that was in Baltimore. It supposedly caters to vampires real well with the top floor just dedicated to us. He said he'd call me and write me emails. I wasn't going to hold my breath per se'. He asked me to come see him in his city. He told me that Baltimore was a lot busier than Biloxi. I was almost certain that was the truth. He'd have to call me and invite me because I've been known to get a little jealous. Huh-the thought of me falling for Dmitri made me want to laugh.

I was happy that Vivian didn't come with the limo when it came to pick up Dmitri, I also was happy that the Council didn't call him to tell him to join them on their endeavors. I actually felt like the Council did like me, (at least the 2 that mattered-Cal & Vivian.) which was great, that's really the only feeling I could put towards it. And since he didn't have to go out on Monday night, we did go for a hunt. He told me it was exhilarating, I was pleased.

I knew Wendy was coming over tonight so I straighten up the house for a little. For an instant the air got really thick. I froze-he was here I could feel 'his' presence and he was right by my house. I ran to my bed room and grabbed my gun-I got my phone as well and walked to my living room. What the fuck was he doing by my house? Now if I had to fight him so be it-but I know putting a bullet in him would make it easier for him to track down. Damn it; Wendy would be over any second now this wasn't exactly the best thing in my book.

I definitely didn't want Wendy out there with this other vampire so close. I was too late. The doorbell rang when I was flipping open the phone to call her. I walked to the door and flung it open to rush her in but nobody was there. It was the hollow night. The wind was having a field day with the brush in my yard. It could be a parlor trick maybe? I stepped out walked a couple steps and look around the front yard, he was sneaky. I turned around and got the door shut again-I leaned on it. I was breathing hard-I was a little uneasy. As I flipped open the phone again to call Wendy the doorbell rang again. I was sick of this fuckers games, I opened the door and jumped out rushing my gun out in front of me, Wendy screamed.

"Wendy." I said.

"What the hell Cat, are you trying to give me a heart attack" She looked scared. "Please get your gun out of my face?" She snorted out pretty angry. I couldn't say anything.She was completely red-she must have gotten a good scare.

"No of course not love, but please let's get inside."I rushed her inside and she came in looking a little teary eyed.

"Can you please tell me what is going on?"She asked me. I took the things out of her hand and walked them to the kitchen, she followed. I wanted her to forget it, but I knew that it wouldn't get dropped.

"It really isn't anything, I just felt his presence." I said it softly.

"Get out of here, here?" she said fast. I nodded yes, I didn't dare speak it any more, I wasn't quite sure if he was here listening to our conversation or not.

"I'm not sure what to make of it. He's never shown his self here before-you know it's probably nothing to worry about." I started thinking this was the best time to cut the plant life away from the fence to utilize the gate in the manor a little better. I had so much plant life in front of my house I was surprised any one could find it. I didn't have any number on my house either. I guess maybe something inside me didn't want to be known or found which only bothered me that much more since this fucking vamp made his self-known to me at my place of refuge.

"I'm glad I made it here when I did then, I didn't see any one out there." She relayed to me.

I was happy she didn't see anyone lurking around my house but I was sure that this vampire was a lot smarter than that. He let her come in-in one piece so he wasn't violent or at least not yet. I hoped she felt safer in the house with me because I should be able to keep her safe. She brought me some blood and a bottle of vodka. I fished out a cigarette packs and threw her the ones she smoked and I started to pack the ones she got for me. We both lit up smokes and commenced on smoking in silence.

"I'm sorry; I didn't mean to scare you." I said to her. She looked frustrated. I did feel a little bad. I mean she didn't know her life was in danger from the moment she got out of her car and walked to my front door. I mean besides me jumping out of the front door pointing a gun in her face. We stayed smoking in silence. I didn't feel him any more after that. I just wondered what all of it was about. I had thought maybe he followed Wendy to my house. But he could just follow me after we closed the club. I guess this was fair game to start my search for him. I needed answers and I'll get them out of him if it's the last thing I do.

After we got relaxed again we started to drink wine together. She really was said and whining about this vampire poker player she was hung up on. They spent a week together when he was in town last time. Ivan Lucas world renounce poker player. He was the best at the game. She lusted him a lot more than her other suitors she came about with. She actually didn't pursue any other gentlemen-She just wanted her Ivan.

She wanted to know about Dmitri. I told her briefly that it was fun and I'd like to get to know him again. I am really not one for kissing and telling. I did say it was nice to have a gentleman's company since I hadn't had one for the longest of times. She just smiled at me with a big smile. I'm not going to lie-I was wondering who this god damn vampire was that decided to come and stalk around me house. How could he end up by my house but never show his face to me.I didn't like this situation-not on little bit.

CHAPTER 5

I GOT UP THAT DAY at sun down-I swear I don't even have to worry about the sun any more but I still never took chances. I peeked out through my window and seen the reds and oranges in the sky. I stretched and shut the blinds-I did the normal routine and jumped into the shower. I usually took a shower after work but I take them before work to. It must be out of habit. It's like grabbing a coat on a winter day. I definitely didn't need one. After my shower I dried my hair which was a task all in itself. I have the longest hair. I rubbed lotion all over my body and placed some make-up on. Spritz some perfume-grabbed my bag than looked out the window; Dark-Perfect.

When I got to the club the valet boys were fooling around they all straighten up when I jumped out of my truck. The all told me hello in unison. It always made me want to laugh because it almost sounded like a boy choir. I went through the doors and the door man that takes admissions nodded to me. I smiled at him. I was in a good mood. When I walked deeper into the club I seen Tony behind the bar and he looked as he was scolding the bar tender. Tony could really be a S.O.B. but that was good no one ever tried to take advantage of him and when he was in a good mood and being nice they knew it was only going to be for a short amount of time.

I remember when I was introduced to him in the early 1990's. Trevor Belmont is who introduced me to him. I knew Trevor since the early 1700's I told him I wanted a legit way to make an income and he brought me Anthony. He's a great business partner. I wouldn't want any other person besides him, he made us money.

"How was your week Catherin?" He asked as he walked toward me. We stood near the stage.

"Relaxing, and yours, how was business?" I answered back.

"It ran like a well oil machine." He purred to me. I was glad to hear that. I was glad to hear there wasn't any trouble. That of course is the best thing to hear as a business owner of any business.

"Catherin, are you going to go off and change into a costume?" He grunted to me.

"Don't I always my friend?" I relayed back to him.He was grumbling something under his breath.

"You don't have to do that, you're their boss-you don't have to dress like one of the dancers." Aw he wanted to take the fun out of it for me.

"Would you really take that fun away from me Tony? Don't you know I like to be one of the girl's, I don't dance I just play bouncer." I smiled to him.

"Well you don't have to dress in those costumes to do it." He was being stubborn, even though we had this conversation at least once a week, he just never gave up. Before I thought it was going to be a good start of the night, Tony started to complain about not letting him know about the Council on Sunday, I really hated doing this but I didn't have gloves on and Tony was for my taking, I place my hand on his shoulder, a little glamour never hurt anybody. In a soft voice I whispered into his ear,

"Anthony-Don't worry about me tonight, also be nice to everyone you come in contact with. After I'm done speaking to you-you'll go to your office and do some work; later tonight you'll lock up the club and go home to your wife." Shame on me!As I let him go he shook his head and looked around like he was dazed.

"I better get into my office; I have plenty of work to do." He said it with conviction; so I was hoping telling him to stay in his office and 'do work' will inspire him to do our overdue books. We walked into the back together he parted from me and headed back to his office. I just walked into the dressing room area. Wendy saw me and smile and came up fast to give me a hug. She smelt good tonight. My girls always put some sort of body lotions on. That's defiantly a strip club smell a barrage of different perfumes and lotions.

"Got to go I'm on stage. Talk to you in a bit." Wendy said in a hurry.

It was Friday night and I had the normal girls in. There were only 25 of them right now-so it looked like I'll be getting a lot of extra rent for the girls that were late. (I charged them for being late and extra 100 bucks) As I scanned the girl's heads it was a bunch of mix emotions tonight. I got money-envy-money-one was worried about her tampon string popping out of her G-string. The all smiled to me and greeted to me but I knew all too well that they were nice because they knew what I was and what I could do if they didn't play nice they all kind of loathed Wendy since she was my friend and favorite.

We had a nice establishment-it was higher class place than anything else. We only went topless-I could have opened a fully nude one but then I wouldn't be allowed to serve alcohol. The girls knew they didn't have to show their breast if they didn't want to-I even had pasties if they wanted to cover them. None of them wore them ever. I guess they were all exhibitionist.

I decided to get dressed in the dressing room tonight. Wanted to be nosey and see what was in all my girls head. Also when the laid eyes on me they seemed to work a lot harder and not stand by the bar and bitch about things. Usually they got more drink tickets when I dressed in the dressing room with them. Drink tickets were like their get out of jail free card. If you get 10 you could change a day on your schedule. If they missed a day and didn't call in it cost 50 drinks tickets. Or 200 bucks. The girls usually gave me their tickets. It was 20 tickets if they came in late. If they didn't have any I even would let them work to get them that same night but if they didn't get enough they'd owe me. I swear drink tickets was a brilliant idea. It cost 20 dollars for their drink no matter what they got. It came in a certain glass and I didn't feed them that much alcohol. They'd get half a shot and the rest would be soda. If they ordered water it come from the tap and still cost 20 bucks. The drinks tickets are something they also hustled to get and people would buy them 20 dollar drinks. It was sheer genius on my part because it just made me that much more money.

I got undressed and stood in the nude. I sucked in all the girls' stares. They all sucked in perfection. I am about 5'7 I have curves but boyish hips. I was thicker woman though to say the least. I had bigger breast and on a good day I could get into a double D bra. I have long dark hair that comes passed the bottom of my butt. My eyes were a greenish brown. My face was a young face-big eyes small nose my lips were on the thicker side. I had a very innocent face-even though I was made when I was 25. When I looked through my bag I notice none of the girls weren't moving or getting the fuck on the floor. I put my hands on my hips and looked around the room.

"I am going to have to be fining you ladies? Get fucking with it." I said with my voiced raised so they knew I wasn't fucking around. The ones that were dressed all started saying sorry and hurrying out the door. The other girls that were still getting dressed got back to work on their hair and faces and getting into their clothes.

I finally decided on a nice white robe type dress. It tied in the front and was long sleeved. It was pretty I thought. The thongs that went with it were really cute with a bow right in the thong part. I usually pack at work but not my 19 11's. Those big girls were strictly a shoulder holster type a gun. I packed one of my 22's at work. I had a nice little thigh holster that is easy to disguise by just putting a garter around it. None of the girls ever asked me about it and I know no customer would ever say anything to me about it. I did have bouncer in my club. They were mostly there because they liked to date stripers more than anything else. I went through them fast to. It seemed like no one stuck around for too long. Wendy-well Treasure here made her way back into the dressing room with a bunch of money clutched in her hand. She smiled and threw all of the bills in front of me on the makeup table.

"It's going to be a good night I can feel it." She was sincerely excited.

Wendy was a good companion-really she was. After Dmitri visit I realized that I'd love a man's companionship as well. I can't lie to you I thought about turning Wendy more and more every day. I don't know if I could stand to be alone again for the years to come. This presence I felt had me always curious to see if he'd be my savoir; but to be honest with you he'd probably be my demise. It's hard to say. But like I said before turning Wendy started to seem like a better idea the more years she stayed close to me as a friend.

Tonight seemed like any other Friday night. I was sitting at the bar next to the stage. I had my eyes on the floor and the girls giving dances. In an instance the air got thick again. Before I could come too to put thought to it he stepped in. I looked onto his face. His eyes were dark and his face was beautiful. He was a bigger gentleman-almost gladiator like. He had broad shoulders and big hands. He was about 6'1-6'2. Curly brown hair that cradled his face sweetly his jaw was strong and had an unbelievable straight nose. His lips were thick and he was also olive skin color and I thought that was so lovely. He was here standing in my club. This was the vampire I had been sensing. I couldn't believe he was here. He approached the main seating area and he placed his eyes on me. I felt so venerable-like I was his prey and for his taking. He made his way to a seat and sat down. The girls immediately started to approach him and he turned them down politely one by one but kept his eyes on me. When he turned down Wendy I had to know what and why he was here. I was a little relived that he showed his self finally. There would be no need to go hunting him now. I got up and walked to him.

"Hello, I have a feeling you're here to see me. I'm Catherin, the

Lady of the house." I said politely. He looked at me softly, at first I had to think if I spoke English or not, then I started to think maybe he didn't.

"You are her." He said in an excited tone. "You loneliness had called me and I had to place a face to it." He said it so softly like he knew who I was and was whispering me a secret. If I were human I probably wouldn't be able to hear it in the club so loud. I was a bit embarrassed to, my loneliness god that made me feel really venerable. Then again maybe that's why Dmitri was so eager to know me, because he sensed I was lonely.

"Where are my manners?" I got stiff and defensive he stood up and pulled out the seat next to him. I sat down and he sat back in the seat he initially was in.

"Among my many names I am Dante." He smiled. When he did it that it was with his mouth and his eyes, his whole face seemed to light up and greet me. People vampire I see. I smiled back to him and it seemed to please him.

"It's a pleasure. Not many of us come in. I'm the main attraction usually and now I feel you've given them more of a show. I should charge double at the door right now." He gave a big hearty laugh.

"A business woman I see." I nodded.

"It's only my lively hood. I have to survive." I answered softly.

"For some reason I don't believe that for one second." He said it like 'matter of fact'. I wasn't sure why I wanted a business out in the open with many humans. I personally think I had a business working with woman to see how things change through time. Also keep contact with my own sense of humanity-and the ladies of the night. Since we were out I could have this club as long as I wanted. I smiled again at him.

"So what exactly brings you into Pandora's Box tonight?" He paused for a second.

"You bring me into Pandora's box tonight." He said it so pleasingly, I was intrigued.

"May I call you Dante?"

"Of course, Catherin is it?"

"Dante, I'm not trying to be rude but I'm here, you've meet me. You're still sitting here, what's the deal-really?" I lifted a brow and went for a cigarillo out of my clutch. He pulled a lighter out and lit it for me.

"This is going to sound absurd, but I have to know you. You let your presence be felt far and long. I had to find a face to place with the presence. Now I just want to explore you more. You don't put a cover on your presence, you must be very sure of yourself and the power that you have." He looked very curious. Did I have a curious vampire on my hands? I couldn't really tell yet-this was going to be interesting.

"You'll have to excuse me if I'm a little shocked. Usually vampires are not so eager to go off and make friends with another vampire unless they want something for their selves. I can't sense your motives so you're very old as well-or you can mask your intentions." I said it calmly. I didn't need to get upset because someone told me that I come off as a cocky vampire because I didn't mask my presence by a long shot.

"No pressure. We can go at your own pace." He blinked. Totally human thing to do, we so didn't need to blink. We didn't even need to move or breathe, everything is out of habit. I could tell he had been living with humans for a very long time.

"Okay let's do say we get to know each other. What would we gain for having each other's company?" I asked he lifted a brow.

"Maybe a companionship for one; there really isn't anything I can say we will gain. Maybe to know another vampire and have company of each other; that's gaining a lot more than what I have now-I could even include you in the statement as well." He said and I'm not going to lie I was extremely intrigued. So I looked at his beautiful face and his thick eyes lashes his wild curls and let his aura fill me with this harmonious feeling. With everything in blowing in the wind I decided to open up a part of me I haven't dared to explore in one of the longest times.

"Yes, let's do get to know each other." After I said it he smiled.

CHAPTER 6

HE WAS SO PERFECT looking. I just couldn't believe that he was sitting in front of me. His face was so hard to read. But I was willing to take a chance on him. I just thought my maker would throw a fit at this very moment, made me wonder where Gabriel was in the world.

"I'm here during the weekend's days but if you'd like to meet soon we can on Monday."Wow, I was feeling less sure of myself the more I talked.He looked at me with his big brown eyes. They looked so comforting.They surrounded me with warmth-this could be a very bad thing.

"Sounds wonderful, how do you propose we do this? We exchange numbers am I correct?" Dante asked?I was already going into my clutch for a business card and got to writing the essentials on them, I hadn't done this that much but I knew the basic's.

"Here are the clubs numbers and my cell number, I wrote my address on the back." Was it over kill, I mean he asked me how we do it, would he know if I was over doing it, was I over doing it?

"When do you rise?" That wasn't something you ask a vampire you just meet. I hope he doesn't take offense.

"Well I usually get up around sundown." He said.He seemed pleased with the card. I was hoping he wasn't some sort of powerful wizard or warlock. Let him just be a legit vampire please. Anything more and I would give my life for the stupidity that was overtaking over me right now.

"How about when you've gotten up and to my place we can order some take out or delivery?" You can order people to come to your house and feed on them now of days. The craigslist and newspapers were the best places to order people from. Also from 'Humans2Go', that's a place you order humans by the whole. It was expensive but you get them by the hour and by blood type. It was something good to get if you were having a party and supplying the evening dinner.

"I don't like to order out-I'll pick up some blood if you want. Which type would you like?" I was setting up a date. I just couldn't believe it. With an older vampire that had been letting me feel his presence for months. This is so not in my character, but after the week I just had with Dmitri-I was wondering what my character actually was?

"I don't have a favorite type, blood is blood." I was being series. Food was food to me. The synthetic blood all tasted the same. That's why I really liked going out hunting.

"Okay, I'll be there on Monday at sundown, but for right now may I get one of those tables in the back over there? I see another man back there with 3 woman and two bottles of champagne." I don't know what Dante wanted, but at that very moment I wasn't thinking it had anything to do with my company. I started to get up. He grabbed my hand.

"Where're you going?" he asked in a small protest.

"I'm going to get you some girls to choose from." I said.

"No, may I not take you tonight? I want to show you that I'm 100% interested." He was smiling softly at me again.

"You really don't have to. You'll get me for free on Monday. Those tables are 300 an hour." I relayed back to him.

He was in a nice suit so it wasn't that I think he couldn't afford it. I knew we could take advantage of each other in my place of business and have our way with each other. I guess I didn't know why it would be a bad idea for us to go sit in the champagne section. I was making an excuse. I needed to relax I started thinking. He smiled, I was happy to see he could keep humor with me being so uptight-or maybe he heard all the indiscretions and doubt and confusion that was going on in my head.

"The best bottle of champagne, with the best bottles of synthetic blood, I'll mix them together and the alcohol goes down nicely. Do you drink?" He said so calmly.

"Are you sure you are ready to spend that kind of money. You don't have much time. We close at 2am." I was curious on why he wanted to have a drink with me. Did he want me drunk?

"I have been sensing you for some time now. I would only feel that a woman of olden ways like your self would have a drink with me. Please have a drink with me?" He asked so nicely, than he lifted his hand waiting for me to take his in my own. I reach down hesitant, but I grabbed his hand. I walked him carefully to our high roller table, or did he walk me, it's hard to say.

"The gentleman wants the platinum package." I relayed to the host of the High Roller section. Before I could make it to the table Wendy intercepted.

"Are you going to introduce me to your friend?" I smiled at my smiling friend.

"Treasure this is Dante, Dante Treasure." Wendy lit up like a freaking Christmas tree. She looked at him and with a nod of the head.

"Please it's Wendy." She relayed back to my mysterious man. Dante looked amuse

"Well Miss Wendy if you don't mind I'd like to talk to your friend Catherin here for a little bit." She smiled so big, it was creepy.

"Okay." She said. She was beaming.I know she was a friend but are they always supposed to act like crazy people when a man comes into the picture? I sure didn't act like that when she was off gallivanting with Ivan.

After the little interlude the drinks came and we had our first glass of champagne. I only knew from experience not to over drink the first time you meet someone. If you begin to weep there are many people left to kill. If you get to excited you could end up crushing someone's skull by accident. But tonight hopefully wouldn't go to that extreme. After my second glass I was feeling lovely.

"May I touch you hand?" He asked as he reaches for mine with his masculine hands and starts to take my glove off.

"Wait, what are you doing?" I knew I shriek it. Listen after what happen with Dmitri I had to think what the fuck was going on.

Having bare palms together with another vampire can be very dangerous. You can Dream Lock so much easier. I wear gloves for other reason besides thinking I'm going to Dream Lock with another of my kind. Dream Locking is a way to lockinto each-others past memories and thoughts. It's very intense. It's the ultimate way to see someone's past. I was just too weird, especially after Dmitri Dream Locked with me, not purposely-but then again I didn't ask him.

"No Dream Locking, to private?" He breathed it out in the form of a question. I was worried.

"What's up Mr. Dante? What do you want? What are you looking for?" I was starting to get upset.

"I have many things I want to share with you. But I want to make sure you're ready to take it all in. This goes against all the rules I've ever set in the past, but I'm looking for a companion. Maybe you could fulfill the void?" What was this vampire's motive really? I was extremely shocked. Did Anthony set me up? Did Wendy set me up? Did he hear my thoughts? Was he for real? I swallowed the rest of my champagne and got the bottle, empty. Damn.

"Waiter, get another bottle-This one is on the house." He shook his head with acceptance and ran off like a good earned boy.

"It looks like it will be a long night till 2. But no Dream Lock tonight, it would be too much, and I also don't want my employees to see me in that state." He looked like he understood. "Monday we can. Alsoplease bring whatever you feel would be necessary to have a comfortable evening at my house." I relayed it to him. He gave me a nice smile.

The rest of the night went smoothly we sat close to each other and spoke just inches from each of our faces. We talked about all the wonderful things we lived through. The French Revolution the many Civil Wars we experienced throughout time. The rise and fall of many rulers he was well lived and well mannered. I hoped it wasn't all a façade. We didn't talk too much about the time now. I guess in some sort of way we didn't want to see the bigger picture that was our lives now and that we were living. When the club was starting to shut down I walked him to the door inside the club. He pressed his lips softly against my cheek and it sent a warm rush through the limbs of my body. After he left I went to my normal routine in the club. Tony was handling the night affairs tonight so I slipped out the back door. I took the long way home tonight I wanted to keep myself on cloud nine.

When I got home I had 2 missed calls from Wendy's cell phone. After I threw off my shoes I heard a knock at the door and the phone ring again. Hmm I wonder who that could be. I didn't have to look through the peep hole, I knew it was Wendy. I could sense her busy head buzzing on the other side of the door. I opened it wide and she was immediately asking questions. She did have a 6 pack of blood and some cheap wine coolers type of drinks 2bottles. She walked past me and I just watched her come right in and make herself at home. 'Yes, please come in I thought.'

"Dante is the person you've been sensing huh? He's so hot. Like what is he?" I was wondering she was talking about what is he? Besides the most beautiful vampire I've ever seen.

"Well he's a very old vampire. What do you mean what is he?" I wasn't thinking correctly. I was still high from our meeting. He had been on my mind for the longest now.

"Never mind, what did you guys talk about? Is he going to start seeing you? Vampires date right? Like are you guys going to do it?" I started to laugh. She was like a little kid with excitement and I haven't even given any thought about what Dante and I will do.

"I have no clue Wendy I just met the man tonight." She had been in the kitchen and when she came around the corner she had a bottle of blood in one hand and was balancing the two bottles of Boones in the other. The Boones was a plus this did call for a celebration.

"If you guys fuck, I want to know all about it. I haven't seen guy vampires in a little while, except those Council members but they don't count because they don't come in and spend money so I guess it's been since last poker tournament. Since Ivan had been in town, that was like a month and some change ago." She said and she was right. We barely did get any vampires in the club, beside the Council. They didn't come in enough to count though.

"I guess I'll share whatever I'm willing to when the time is here. For now we are just going to get to know each other." She looked disappointed.

"You don't have to wait long to know each other, don't you have to hold each other hands and know everything there is to know? Doesn't it work like that?" I know that Wendy wasn't the average woman-she was actually pretty street smart, and knew remarkably a lot about vampire politics.

"It can work like that but we will see." I wish she'd leave it alone but I had a feeling she'd talk her-self blue in the face before that happened. I reached out to touch her.

"Oh no, none of that Ms. Catherin, I want to remember this conversation." Sometimes it just doesn't pay to have a human friend if they knew your little secrets. "Any ways you'll want to talk to someone about the mysterious Dante." Her eyes were big. Her excitement was contagious. I felt it all over me tingling and pinching. Well I guess she'll be nice to talk to after the fact.

CHAPTER 7

It was early Monday night. The sun still was out when I rose.I could feel its heat up above. I wonder how things will go tonight. I could smell the flowers in the garden outside. I was glad to have hired people to come and clean and keep up my property. Of course my bedroom had the windows blacked out, but I also had the other two bed rooms with the bathrooms blacked out to. Wendy's bed room had its windows blacked out. My coffin room didn't even have windows. I don't like sleeping in a coffin unless I absolutely have to. I prefer my big king size bed and my many pillows.

I got up, I showered and after that I felt like I smelled perfect. I decided on some yoga shorts and tank top. I walked around my house and lite candles and incense and open up my heavy curtains. I opened my French-doors that led out to the back yard. The smell of the garden entered the house. I hope Dante would like the freshness of the flowers and plants.

After I did a little straitening up, there wasn't much to do my house is usually always clean, the doorbell rang. I didn't need to look out the peep hole because I could sense him like the burning sun above. It was that presence that always haunted me and now he was going to be my guest tonight. I opened the door fast and smiled at him. Dante was there with his hands full.

"Can I help you with some of that stuff?" Remember to invite him in I thought.

"Hello Catherin. There's no need, but I'd love it if you pointed me to a table or the kitchen." He remarked back to me.

"Ok sure-'Please come in.'" I remembered, brownie points for me. I hurried him into the house and led him to the kitchen. I wondered what will concur with having this vampire guest in my house. He's the 2nd one this month. This was some sort of new record for me. I started asking myself why I brought him here. I could have met him at a hotel. But that seems so cheap, even to me. That's what you do to a date you don't want anything to do with. Take them somewhere they can't contact you back at. No ties with them.

Dante had nice pants on-he fit them really well. A nice fitted shirt his curls were a little messy on his head but they weren't frizzy. He had newer sneakers on. I could see his nipple shape through his shirt since it fit so tight. All his muscle were strong under it to-his chest his biceps. Even his forearms were nice and strong looking.

"So what are you planning tonight Dante? It is our first date, but I'm sure we don't have to follow the same rules." I was wondering if there were rules, I also was hoping that Dante would acknowledge that we were having our first date. It made me think if it's what me and Dmitri experience'the 1st date?'

"Like I told you before no pressure, I don't really mind for the night just to pass and we surround our self with nonchalant chat or if we just stay in silence. It's another vampires company that I am in the mood for, and having company with someone as stunning as you. Well that my dear is a plus that I can't deny I'm improving on." He said so calmly.

I smiled, I really shouldn't believe him and his compliments, we are the masters of deceit so now only time will tell how sincere he really is. His presence was even stronger in person. He gave you a warm comfort feeling. I wasn't so sure if it was a parlor trick or what. It felt like I was connected to him already. I didn't know why I had this feeling with him. But it felt like the beginning and how I felt connected to my maker.

Dante had his way around the kitchen. He pulled out to big stem-less wine glasses. I smiled I was happy there wouldn't be any balancing a wine glass around where ever we go if we were going to get drunk that made me a little excited to. I felt spunky so blurted in French.

"Languesquesavez-vous?"

"I speak all languages-I'm certain there are some tribal culture languages I don't know but I know the basics of all the others." He said to me. He seemed to be comfortable at my place. That was good. I wanted him to feel at home. I relayed to him the importance it was to me for him to feel comfortable.

"Please I'd like you to make yourself comfortable. Remove your shoes-I'll go make a fire." I went and laid out a tiger rug I had. It was old; I think at least 200years old. It surprises me to see that the fur still stuck to the skin but I usually always skinned my pets well enough for the skin to last for a small eternity.

Before I even could think he was shoeless and shirtless, (glad he really made his self-right at home.) he had no belt on either, which made me think did he actually have one on? I was more than impressed with the half-naked man that was in front of me. Could a man look that perfect? Like a Greek statue in ancient Greece. I smelled the drink it was an older Absinthe and blood. He glanced at the rug.

"Nice. Big cats always made for a good skin. He's old I can see around the edges. But they sure do last." He was kneeling down and petting the rug like it was still the big cat I had got him from.

"Absinthes, this night is going to be a night to never forget." I smiled; I haven't drunk absinthes for the longest of time.

"Come and sit in front of the fire. You don't have to drink it if you don't want to. No pressure." Dante said I looked in his eyes. He looked at home. He didn't seem to have a worry in the world. Then what would a vampire as old as him worry about.

He guided me to the rug and guided me to a sitting position. We just stared at each other for a while, in our own little eternity.

After about half an hour I started to feel the effects of the absinthes. This was good absinthes. Usually you couldn't find the good stuff anymore. It doesn't exactly make you hallucinate but it makes you feel like everything around you is alive. You see every things aura, or at least feel it. Like I know the cat we were sitting on was dead and just made a rug, but in an instance it seemed like it was purring.

"Do you want to start?" He paused, "Did you want to Dream Lock?" He lifted one of his palms to me palm out. I just gathered a breath and thought to myself-Here goes nothing.

I sat up straighter and placed my palm on his. Than instantly we were connected. I was tingling and hot like I was on fire. I was traveling in a bright tunnel. At the end I saw Dante. He looked exactly the same. He was in a great big garden. It was beautiful, green and full of plants and flowers. I could smell the flowers and I was reaching out to touch them. He was gathering them in a big basket and he was walking. I had Dante in my hand still and we followed his Dream Lock form to an altar. He placed these beautiful fruits and beautiful wheat's and flowers that smelled so sweet with perfume that I just thought it was perfect.

Then I see another young man come. He was blonde-his facial features were similar, he had blue eyes. He brought a young sheep with him. The baby sheep was crying to and resisting. They lay their gifts there. The other young man slit the sheep's throat and let it bleed. Something was happening than. It got so very dark, than very cold.

We enter the tunnel of light again. Then we were in my time and I saw the same thing I did before in the Dream Lock with Dmitri, I open the door to the knock. I remember how sorry I felt for them to get caught in the heavy rain. How I didn't want the man or the dog to get stuck out there. I knew they'd end up getting into more trouble than now, with flooding being so common. How naïve I was. I had seen enough and I let go. We came to, and I was glad to see my living room again. I was making the act of breathing hard.

We sat there looking blankly at each other for a while. A long while maybe an hour. It was fine to me. I was feeling the absinthes. We stared at each other and got lost in each other eyes, well at least I got lost in his.

"Please forgive my actions. But I have to do this." Dante whispered to me so sensually. I was thinking what would you be sorry about?

He approached me and placed his arms around my waist. He leaned in and touches my lips with his very softly. He really didn't have to be sorry about this I wasn't going to stop this I thought it was a good idea. I pushed a little harder into his lips and he opened my mouth with his and pressed his tongue in me very softly. He was gentle while we embraced in our kiss. He started to try to get off my shirt and I helped my taking it over my head. He stood me up and pulled off my shorts he just looked up at me and I guided him to stand with me I got on my knees and worked off hit pants as well. He was one for not wearing undergarments as well so needless to say I was met with a very happy man part. I looked at his lower naked body he was absolutely perfect extremely endowed and totally erect. He got on his knees and laid me down on my rug I could feel the heat from the fire and hear the cracking of the wood. He leaned down and stroked my breast with his hand sucking on them my nipple that was already hard from his breath. He laid me completely back and went down to my legs-opened them so gentle. He got to my pubic hair and smiled. He pushed with a little more force so I could spread open my sex to him. He kept his eyes on me and opened my lips with his hand. The knot in my legs started to throb hard. He pressed his tongue on it and I let out a moan. He grabbed my lower body into his mouth and was doing intense circles. He pushed his finger in me and tried to sit up but he rushed me down again. He lifted me gentle with each stroke he pushed in me. He kissed my thighs and came up with his kissing to my face. He locked into my eyes and inserted his self into my sex. I could feel it get wetter with his thrust inside of me. He placed his arms behind my back and held my shoulder and pushed me down with each stroke up. I moaned loud with the first stroke. We were kissing and moving our bodies. I was breathing. It felt like I was breathing him in, him and all the power he possessed behind him. His power, his old soul, his agelessness ran through my body. He sat up a little and stuck his thumb on the knot in the middle of my legs. I let out another moan. I started to feel hot and before I could protest he thrusts hard into me and my yell of victory was stolen in silence. He had my waist in his hands and thrusts inside of me hard once again. I shivered against him and he was kissing my stomach softly. We were still one with each other. After a moment we lay next to each other looking onto each other's face. I laid there thinking of my whirl wind life for the last couple of weeks, not having any men company for the longest than two all rushed into together. I stood up.

"Where're you off too?" Caine said, sounding a little hurt.

"I'm getting a cigarette my dear, did you want one?" I smiled, man could I smile, I know that if my smile were lights at that moment I probably could blind the angels.

"Yes." Caine said. I didn't have to go far. They were right above the fireplace. I grabbed two smokes and grabbed my Fabre shay egg lookalike, it was a lighter. I gave him one and he pulled me down to rest in his arms.

"I'm sure since you drank absinthes with me you wouldn't object to some other party favors? You're an owner of a gentlemen's club, I'm sure you know all about it." Well that got me thinking that Dante would fit right at home with me and Wendy but it also started making me think of my Council member friend Dmitri. Why at a moment like this I would think of him but I did. I wonder if Dmitri did do anything else but drink. I'm almost certain he does since he's also an owner of a club. Huh.

"So what do you have in mind?" I asked trying to stop my pointless thinking. He went to get his pants and from them he pulled out a little baggie. They had four pills that were peach color in a bag. I would presume they were ecstasy. He must know me very well.

"I'll have to admit to you Dante. I don't usually do drugs on the first date or drink Absinthe. But you seem so relaxed please tell me you don't drug your victims?" I asked and laughed a little since I was half teasing. He winked at me.

"No, nothing like that, usually they don't give up a fight." He said calmly. Of course they didn't when I came to think of it. How could anyone turn down a man that looked as beautiful as him? I know I couldn't, hence the reason why I was laying naked on my cat rug. I just smiled in the friendliest and sexiest way I could. When I really put any thought to it I thought why not. He was my guest and I didn't want the night to end for sure. I smiled and nodded yes. So he handed me one. I wondered where my clothes were and how many pieces they were in.

"Who was the man in the Dream Lock?" he asked me.

"Who was the young man at the altar?" I asked back. We both looked at each other.

"He was my brother." I just took a breath remembering I didn't have to pretend but since we were getting to know each other.

"That was my maker." We were quiet. I lay down and he lay next to me on his elbow. The pills didn't take that much time to kick in. Maybe it was because of the absinthes. It was hard to say. I started to get tingly in my back and it sent in shiver in me and hardened my nipples. Caine seemed to notice I started to feel the effects of the pills because he placed his arm around me and cradled me in his arms.

"We will take our time. Let us just lay here and be together as only vampires can be." I couldn't deny that I didn't want to.

"Then you'll stay with me tonight." I said.

"Of course I will. I would hope after we experience something like that you wouldn't turn me away." I rubbed his head full of loose curls and we started to kiss again. I could feel my body harden under his kiss and the hard throb in my legs start. He smiled at me I'm sure he sensed it. We let the things go where they were destined to go. I can't lie I needed it and to be completely honest this was all right with me.

CHAPTER 8

TUESDAY CAME-IT ROSE LIKE I knew it would. I rolled over to a big beautiful man next to me. My new lover lay there so peaceful. I started feeling extremely grateful that it wasn't some sort of crazed drug induce dream. I rolled out of bed being gentle and went to put clothes on. I usually never wear under garments but I thought I could wear a nice bra and pantie set I had. I was black and had red laced on the edges of it. It was silk and extremely sexy. I pulled on a pair of blue jeans and thought to myself even though my house was clean my closet was a mess. I walked to the living room and found the pieces of my clothes from last night. Wow-it didn't seem that we were that eager last night but the clothes were ripped and unfixable side so I just placed them in the trash. I started to wonder where Dante laid to rest when he wasn't out swooning woman.

I walked over to my wooded blinds and opened them for a peek. I was happy to have remembered to close the French-doors last night before we retired for the night. When I peeked out it was pink and red skies like always. I felt Dante's presence and turned around to be met with him close to my body. He smiled at me and leaned into my face and kissed my lips with tenderness. Dante looked so beautiful and gentle. But I knew all too well that neither one of us were gentle.

"I went home when you fell asleep and got some clothes. I hope you don't mind." He was wearing khaki drawstring pajama pants. No shirt. His upper body would make the statues crumble in Europe if they were to see such perfection.

"I don't mind." He was in the kitchen before I could blink heating up some blood for us. I guess he didn't have to pretend with me, I after all was a vampire too. Dante came back he looked lost in thought. His curls were messy on his head but his brown eyes stunned me where I stood.

"Now I don't want you to take offense with this question." He said smiling at me a little.

"That sounds absurd why would I be offended?" I said laughing a little.

"How old are you?" He asked like he earnestly wanted to know. Oh boy this was going to be shocking to him.

"To be completely honest with you Dante, I have no clue." I know how horrible it is not to know how old you are but it's the truth and I wasn't going to start off the relationship lying to my new lover. "When I go about looking it up they send me on a wild chase to a time unknown. So I stop searching. I don't think it matters since I've slept for hundreds of years at a time so I don't think it matters when you get right to it-I am old and lost." I said to him. He lifted a brow. "Lost only sometimes-well most of the time." I wasn't embarrassed because I honestly didn't know the answer to his question.

"Impressive I must say to you. I know that you're an older vampire by your scent alone. Your present is a fun young type mask. It makes you seem younger so it's weird to have you in my presence with your smell and your feel. You're an enigma." He said to me calmly. I never have been called that before. So I just smiled. I couldn't fight and say 'NOI'm not' that would be ridiculous. And he didn't say it to be an insult I didn't think.

The microwave beep and Dante went back to the kitchen. I got up and went over to my office desk. I started to check my email, I heard Dante in the kitchen shaking the blood bottles. I got an email from Vivian; all I could think was joy.

//

Ms. Hope, the bounty list has managed to change since it is forever changing. I put the three main vampires in your area that you should watch out for. If you need to know more about the vampires there are listed in the Council's website archives. Please be sure your safe with the pass word and access for the website. That knowledge could be used against us if some of it were ever to get out.

Vii

1. Derek Chasten
2. Solomon King
3. Trevor Belmont

//

This was not a good thing. My heart dropped. Trevor Belmont was on the list. He was my companion for many years. I couldn't see him doing anything that would cause him to get onto the bounty list. Not by his own doing.

"Are you alright my dear you look flushed." Flushed was the wrong word I thought.

"It's nothing." I closed my laptop. I didn't want my new vampire lover to worry about the thing I should be really worried about more so than falling in love, or lust. I guess it's whichever comes first.

"So would you like to come to my house? Maybe meet my day man?" Dante asked.

"You have someone one to handle your day business for you?" I was thinking maybe I could hire him too. I hired a company to come and tend to my lawn. They weren't even aloud in the house. All they had access to be in was my lawn shed in the back.

"Yes, I caught him when he was a teenager. He was had a

pillow case of mine and he was stuffing contents in it that I'm sure would lead him to some money on the street." He relayed to me. Wow, he caught him stealing and took him in. This vampire is a savoir or really smart. I know that he has to have giving some sort of blood exchange unless he glamour's him. But that would take so much time. I'm sure he treats this man extremely fair and well.

"That really surprises me? You must have patience or look at every situation as a positive." I said.

"He is my servant. After taking him in, I took care of him and gave him everything that he needed. He learned to trust me and he knows he's allowed to leave anytime he likes. He chooses not to, so I'm sure he likes the arrangement we have. He even started courting a young woman here in the city. She works at the shopping mall here in Biloxi." He raised a brow after saying that.

"Sure let's go meet your day man. May I change before we leave?" He looked at me up and down.

"You don't have to I think you look beautiful. You could even pass as human with your dress." I smiled.

"Let me place some glove on though." He gave me a hard look and I walked back to the bedroom. I went into my glove drawer and got out a pair of white ones that didn't have fingers in them so they were fingerless gloves and it still worked so I didn't mind. I walked out to the living room pallor area and I smiled and lifted my hand. He just smiled. We were exciting the door and my house phone rang. I just rushed to the phone.

"Hello?" I said. I knew it was Wendy by the caller ID.

"Cat!" Wendy blurted to me. She sounded so excited it made me want to start laughing.

"Yes love, how arc you?"

"How was your night?" Wendy asked really extenuating your night.

"To be complete honest with you it hasn't ended yet." I could feel her smile emanate through the phone.

"Okay, I'll let you go. Call me as soon as you can." She giggled to me.

"Yes of course. Talk to you later." She hung up, no good bye-eh that's okay I guess. We got to the point. I looked at Dante. He did have a lot of patience.

"Sorry it was Wendy, she knew we had a date last night and she extremely nosey." I said. I was a bit embarrassed. He didn't seem to mind one bit. It was almost like he knew what to expect from a human woman.

I walked outside to a Mercedes, SCL600. I hadn't asked him what he did for a living but I'm sure it whatever it was he was making good money doing it. Actually take that back, really good money doing it.

He lived in Ocean Springs over the bridge and further from the shore. His house was triple the size of mine-it was huge to say the least. We pulled up to a gate and he punched in a few numbers and the opened on command. We drove around a circle drive to big white double doors. His house was coral with whited trimmed windows. I wanted to laugh a little-I just couldn't imagine a man of the dead with such a quaint little house. It was almost in some sense charming. I rarely think anything is charming.

He stopped right in front of his massive doors and rushed out the car to open my door. He held out his hand and gathered me right into his grip as soon as I step out of the vehicle. He walked me to his door so swiftly and eagerly I wanted to laugh. He opened the door and I paused; even if I wanted to for the life of me I wouldn't be able to get over the threshold with a proper invitation.

"Please come in." He said so persuasive to me. I stepped in and I was by far blown away. He had a huge foyer that was at least 3stories high. There were stairs that lined either side of the walls going up to substantial sized opening that looked to be the second floor. On the ceiling there was a painting of angels. I thought that was a little odd. Why would he have angels on his ceiling as art we were a little on the peculiar side so there wasn't time to asked questions.

When we walked to the middle of the massive entrance way I saw a younger man walk from down the stairs. He was tall dark and handsome in my eyes. Taller than me with dark skin dark hair and dark eyes his nose was on the wide side but his lips seemed to match his face completely. He smiled and he had extremely straight teeth.

"Catherin, this is Victor. Victor this is Catherin." He studied me, and then nodded.

"Pleasure Catherin, it's nice to see master with a woman as enchanting as you." He had a faint Spanish accent and I really thought he was putting on the charm a little thick. I nodded to him and smiled.

"What is it that you exactly do Dante?" I asked to Dante, I was only curious. Dante came and put his arms around my waist, placed his cheek against mine.

"I dabble in a lot of different things my dear. I mostly do types of banking and agriculture things. I own some produce companies along the coast and around the nation. I also own building across the country but mostly Tri Area South. You know the area I'm sure." He whispered the last bit to me. He still had me firmly in his grip and he leaned me back into a dip. When I met his face again I smiled to him. He began to waltz me around his entrance way. How I would love to have Dante on my arm back in time. I would have been such comedy to see all the women faces. I am sure they would have loathed and envied me that much more than they did. Huh-getting lost in day dreams was so bad for vampires though.

Peeking at Victor and he was watching us softly with a slight smile on his face. When Dante stopped us we were just arm distance from him. Victor quietly bowed and walked back to under the stairs which seemed to be a dining room of some sort. He came back with a parchment envelope with a big red wax seal. He bowed while handing it to Dante.

"These vampires came by last night and dropped this off. I didn't invite them in, I just took the envelope." Victor said sounding like he was going to wait for approval from his master.

"You did well Victor" Dante said. Victor smiled and walked away. He popped the envelope right open. He has obviously had come across waxed letters before. He read and became pleasing happy.

"Catherin our night together and I feel like a young vampire again and it seems the Council will have the hearing; what do you think of me running for king of Tri Area South?" He sounded so commanding. I thought it was a splendid idea. He seemed well lived as a vampire and human alike. I was a bit curious on why he wanted to be only king of Tri Area South and not King of the Council.

"That is a wonderful idea. I couldn't think of anyone else that would be better suited for the position." I quietly bowed to him and he just wrapped his arms around me.

"Then you'll grant me with your company to the hearing?" He asked-or stated; hard to tell with his man he seemed like he could have anybody do anything why me? Should I be worried that he'd like my company at the hearing? The only thing I could think of is Dmitri. Dmitri was Council member but I wasn't even so sure how serious he was with what we experienced. I guess I was some sort of game for the Council. That just made me feel a little used. Since I was putting thought to it I started to get a little upset.

"Are you alright love?" Dante asked sweetly to me.

"Yes completely-I'm just thinking." I lied so shoot me.

"You didn't get a visitor last night-I know since your business the Council deals with you too. Do you not receive letters at your home?" He asked in a very curious fashion. His eyes were opened wide to me. He was a peculiar man certainly.

"No I receive my mail at my club. None of the Council knows where I live." Okay lie two but I'm not going to keep track so don't keep track either.

"We must go to your club I am certain they've invited you

to the hearing as well." He smiled to me this time and ran to his door opening it for me. I did a slight bow and rushed outside. He opened his passenger side door of his car and before any protesting could accrue we were off to my club.

CHAPTER 9

W E GOT TO THE club and I allowed him to park in my space.
He relayed to me I had the best spot in the house. I knew
I had the best parking spot it is my place of business. When we got
through the doors and I had my first glance at Tony he looked like
he'd been up for ages. When he saw me he immediately looked
relieved. He rushed to me and that was a bit odd for him.

"What's up Tony?" I asked this frantic little man. He scrunched
his face to me.

"Don't you answer your phone?" He bellowed to me. He was
angry. "Why even have cell phones if you don't answer it?" I had
left my cell phone at the house. It didn't even accrue to me to bring
it or have it on. I guess I was trying to ignore the world while in
the company of my company. It really didn't accrue to me to have
it on me. He pulled out a letter similar to the one that Victor gave
Dante. I was a bit dumbfounded because this over worked him so
badly. He was an angry poor little man.

"These two big shot vampires came in last night, I had to check
the vampire books I wasn't expecting to see any here. They came
looking for you. Are you in any trouble?" he said to me, sounding
concerned. I just gave him a hard look-he should know I don't get
into trouble. "Well they wanted me to give you this." I wished that
these vampires wouldn't have put Tony in such a sour mood. I felt
bad for my short sweaty partner. I made Anthony register Dante-
which I think he was trying his hardest not to do.

"Anthony, this is Dante." Tony did the sizing up thing and I thought to myself hope he doesn't embarrass himself.

"Dante is it, Anthony." He did the whole pointing to himself with his thumb. Before I let Tony embarrassed himself any further I had to excuse him.

"That's all Anthony thank you for the message." He snorted and scurried off. Dante had my letter open he seemed so pleased.

"It looks that you're invited to the Council meeting as well my love. This will be a pleasant affair it's for two nights on the third weekend of September. You will be able to make it-right?" He seemed so please with my invitation like his own. I started thinking I should be able to make it. Tony understands that the Council is something he has to deal with at least until he retires. Also who would I get to fill in my spot on the weekends? I like having vampire girls on the weekend. For the faint of heart who likes to come in for a little walk on the wild side. Shit-Tony knew some vamp girls that could make their way into the club.

"I should be able to make it. It's a good month away. I'm certain I can find someone to fill my position for the weekend." He was looking around my club. I was hoping he'd stay away from asking me for a tour. If he really got a good look at the place he'd probably see it like I see it. Clubs are kind of dirty. Don't get me wrong we can clean the counters off and vacuum the carpet-but there is something about dirty shoes and smoke that just doesn't want to come out of the carpet and the walls it just all around kind of a shit hole.

"Should we go?" He wanted to leave. I had to talk to Wendy before we went left though.

"Let me go and talk to my little human friend really fast so she doesn't decide to come over tonight after work." He understood. So he let me go off to search for her. She was in a booth doing a dance. I went into the next booth and stood on the chair and looked over to see if I could get her attention.

"Holy shit Catherin-Don't ever do that you scared the piss out of me." I was hoping for the customer's sake that she was using that as an expression.

"That's going to 20 bucks please." The customer handed her the money and left. I got off the chair and went to the booth she was in and sat down. She sat next to me. She was waiting for me to budge first.

"Sowe are going to spend another night together. We might actually be becoming an item." I said to her. She let out a sigh. Then she started with the big creepy grin again.

"Oh my god I can tell you totally had sex was it good?" She began to laugh. "Y'all might be an item now vamps don't waste any time do they I wonder if Ivan likes me than?" She was being Wendy.

"I'm sure he does honey-but he has a lot going on for being a vampire with the poker tournaments." I said trying to reassure her.

"Yeah your right-so was it good?" She gave me the creepy grin she always could muster up.

"It was but we have a lot to learn from each other still. But I'm thinking tonight will be another night of exploration. You wouldn't happen to talk to Daisy still would you?" I asked. Daisy had been Wendy's step sister that she didn't grow up with but ended up meeting after her step sisters after life.

"Yes I do. Why what's up?" Wendy relayed to me. I was actually glad.

"I have to go out of town to Jackson for the third weekend of next month, and I need a vampire for that weekend. I'd need her for maybe 3 days. I'll pay her cash she can get it after the weekend is up." I met Daisy only once, and I didn't care for her-but she was a vampire and I liked having vampires on the weekends she would do just fine.

"Out of town huh? What's in Jackson?" Wendy asked. She was snotty and nosey.

"It's a vampire thing. I'm going to a Council meeting." She lifted a brow, she was a little too curious.

"Can I come?" she asked.

"Sure I don't care, but I got to run." I said back. She smiled. I got up and squeezed her hand. We left the club but not before I went to Tony to hug him. He tried to get away from my advances at first but when I gripped him tight he eventually fell into it. Good for him.

When Dante and I arrived back to my place he looked in thought. I opened my front door. We both walked into the kitchen. I was making blood and he grabbed a beer and gave me one as well. I took my gloves off and just went about my business to get comfortable in the house.

"You said that your descendant of Pandora?" Actually I had briefly mentioned that when we met on Friday. I would have thought he would have forgotten about it. But he seems to remember everything.

"Yes, she would have been my very great grandmother. I'm many generations past her though. I know she was the first woman made besides Lilith and the way our lineage worked it is every first born female carries the Pandora gene. I was the first female born and my mother was the first born before me her mother before her and so on and so forth. I don't have any children so I'm it. I am the last descendant of the lineage." I took a breath. That was a mouth full.

"Is Dante your real name? I only ask because you said it's amongst the many things you're called." I wanted to know the other names he was known as. It was the longest silence that had ever been left with us. Made me wonder if I hit a sour note, I hope this doesn't take us to our first fight it's only our second night together.

"You would find out at the Council and I'm glad you ask." He looked at me softly. "I am Caine." I choked. Vampires don't choke and I choked on my beer. I was completely lost for words. This situation just wasn't fathomable-this can't be 'The Caine'. I thought of all the stories I knew of him in an instant. It just can't be him.

"You can't be Caine." Could he? "You were cursed into Nod for killing your brother." He looked in thought again. But also sadden by my words to him. I didn't want to make him upset or sad.

"It isn't like that at all Catherin, I had to give my first love to him-my brother was my first love my first everything." He had anger in his voice now. But I could tell he was saddened as well. I grabbed his hand and I felt agony despair sadness and over everything else he was extremely lonely. "I am not one to go out of my way to find compassion and understanding and especially love. When Michael made me a Watcher there were rules-my rules. I'm breaking them all now. With you-I want to break all the rules I've ever set out." I wrapped my arms around him and lay my head on his shoulder. I didn't know what to feel. I felt so vulnerable at this moment. Vampires and their romantic nature we are the damned aren't we. "Catherin doesn't seem like a Greek name, does it mean anything?" Caine asked me in a semi whisper.

"It means Pure in Greek my love." I started breathing my heart was beating hard in my chest.

"Pure, that's perfect. I love it, it makes me have hope." I smiled a little.

"Don't be silly. You know my last name is Hope." I said to him he pressed his eye brows together. "You can't be descendant of Pandora without hope in your heart." I guess I didn't give him my last name when we met on Friday. He looked at me and he began to give me a nice calm humming feeling. In that moment he captured my soul in his gaze-I haven't felt so human for my own small eternity of my afterlife. He almost placed me in a trance. I was amazed with how he could make me feel just by looking at me. I smiled. "Yes Catherine hope please to meet you-my king." I whispered to him still locked in his trance.

We didn't speak another word all night long. I made us drinks and walked him to a bath I drew for us. I scrubbed his body down. Rubbing across his chest and back; his arms-his big hands. If this is 'The Caine' he is the beginning. He should have slept through many ages. I would think it would make him mad if it were any other way. But since he was the beginning maybe he didn't sleep through centuries at the time. I knew so many stories of him. It was almost to the point of being unbelievable. Dante was one of Caine's many names. That story must have slipped past me. He was made a Watcher by Michael. That drove me about crazy just thinking of it. He knows all our secrets. I only hoped that he'd share those secrets with me. As long as I lived I still felt so lost in this world. My place as a murderous young woman to lusting after blood and death and now being known to humanity led you to a different path-things just seem to be more confusing all over again. I guess I can be patient-we have nothing but time.

CHAPTER 10

AFTER BEING TOGETHER FOR the week I thought I had all my surprises about everything but today when I opened my eyes I didn't dare to move. There was someone in the house besides me and my vampire lover. He rolled over and put a finger up to his lips. I was thinking yeah Caine of course I'm going to be quiet. Caine walked over to my bedroom door. You could see someone walking around right outside it. As Caine stood by it there was a knock.

"Master, Are you awake yet?" Victor said. I think I might have let out a breath of air, I was breathing-habit.

"It's Victor." He said opening the door. "How did you get in here my dear boy?" Victor looked guilty.

"The back door wasn't' locked." He said almost sounding ashamed.

"What is it Victor?" Caine asked him his butt staring at me, standing naked in front of his day man was just funny to me. I fought my urge to laugh.

"I just wanted to make sure this was the right address. There is no number I could find on the house itself." Caine seemed pleased with his answer.

"Well you've the right place. Let me think what I can get you started with today." He said quickly.

"Well master I can cut the weeds away from the gate so it can close again." Caine lifted an eye brow.

"Catherin, you have a gate?" I was really holding my laughter back now.

"Victor let me take a look at it. I'll see if I can have my day people can help. We will have to make sure we show master here as well." I gathered my blanket around me and winked at Victor who smiled very big. I wasn't so sure if he was smiling because I winked at him, or if it was because I was wrapping myself with my sheet to approach the door. Caine didn't seem embarrassed at all. He ended up dismissing his day man. Victor mentions something about going out tonight.

After getting around of putting a robe on showing Caine the gate, it made me wonder why my workers never asked me if they should cut threw my over grown mess of vines and bush to get to the gate. It looked like a lot of work. After my many unsuccessful attempts to get into the shower, none by my doing, something about being naked around my new lover led to all sort of things except the shower where I wanted to be and go. I decided to call Wendy. He didn't protest any with that action.

"What you doing Ms. Wendy?" I said when she answered the phone.

"Nothing, never mind about coming with you to the Council meeting I have a date. It's Ivanhe got in last night." Wendy said. That's the one she was hung up on. I was glad he was back in town and calling her.

"We'll have to hang out when we're at the Council meeting. It should be fun." I said. I thought she snorted behind the phone.

"Oh, I know Catherin. Ivan likes to party too, he said that he made reservation and a vampire hotel down there and got a mini suite. Where are you staying?" she asked. I wasn't so sure where I was staying yet. I hadn't even asked if Caine had it all set up. We've been together for the week, and it felt like its own little eternity.

"I'll be in touch with you—I'm almost certain he'll be crashing here again tonight so if you want I know you're off tomorrow so if you would like to come over you should. You can meet him." I asked. She was quiet. She was a quiet thinker.

"I had plans with Ivan if it's alright to bring him I can drag him over too." She started laughing.

"That isn't a problem with me love. You two are more than welcome to grace us with your presences." I relayed to her.

"Okay I'll see you two later." She was being a little goofy.

"Yep see you later." I hung up and my brain was on fire. What did I think was going to transpire with bringing over another vampire to my house?

"Caine with the Councilmeeting being just a little bit away you wouldn't happen to set up a place for us to stay because I'd have to get online to handle business." I said smiling at him a little.

"Did you always be so free with your words?" He asked me laughing to his self a little.

"I know I pick up on slang easy. I adapt." We both started laughing after I said that.

"Don't worry love-I made reservations all most immediately after getting the Council invitation. There aren't many suites in the Dae'Moon. The suite I got us has two separate bedrooms and a huge bath room for both rooms. Separate living area. It's a home away from home. I stay in the same room every time I make my way to Jackson." I guess that it was final-we were going as each other's date. I guess I could get Dmitri out of my head.

"Wendy and Ivan are going to come over tonight after she gets off work." I stretched, not sure why, but I just felt like doing it. It felt good too. He was sliding on pants I wanted to protest but he would have to have clothes on for company.

"Is Ivan a human or a vampire?" Caine asked.

"Vampire, he was a guest at the club. I guess they hit it off good. He's going to the Council meeting. He's bringing her as a date." Caine eyes narrowed.

"You wouldn't know if he's Ivan Lucas the vampire poker player?" He asked.

"Yes that's him. He was here for a poker tournament that's how they met each other." He looked pleased.

"If you're worried about her there is no reason to be. Ivan is a good humanitarian to some sense vampire." He said easily.That's good. I wasn't really worried. I worried at first when she said she was going to go out with him. But when she came back with all her stories about how great he was to her the worry quickly faded-anyways he couldn't kill her without me finding him andtracking him down.

"I'm going to go to the store and get some blood. Also some booze." He brought back the empty 6pack of a blood package from the kitchen.

"We could feed off each other, but I don't like sharing so Ivan and Wendy would be out of luck." I said, even though we haven't fed off each other. We haven't exchange blood at all.

"I'll be gone maybe 20minutes tops. Can you see to it you don't get into any trouble while I'm gone." I tried to blink my long eye lashes at him. I left right after that. How much trouble could I get into away from him? I wonder?

CHAPTER 11

I GOT INTO MY TRUCK, practically throwing myself in it since it was so high off the ground. At the store I grabbed a basket walked over to the liquor section and picked up a two big bottles of vodka. Then I walked back to pick up some blood. I grabbed two 6 packs of blood. I wasn't really paying any mind but these two girls were whispering into each other's ear and staring at me. Hmm curious are they. I decided I could have a little fun. I disappeared behind the aisle and kept my eyes on them. They looked confused. I heard the one she was almost in a panic,

"Where did she go? She was just here." This is going to be even more fun that I was initially thinking. I placed down my basket and ran and pushed the taller one into the shorter one.

"What was that?" She was frantic now. I picked up my basket again and went to stand in the line. They emerged from the back of the store. The taller one looked almost a nice shade of green. That should have been a lesson well learned. But you never can put it by humans these days.

I got the things in the truck and pulled off. I notice a blue Toyota following me. How wonderful, I get to have a little more vampire fun. I flipped open my phone and dialed my house. I wondered if Caine would be smart enough to answer the phone. He was,

"Hello, Ms. Hope's residents."

"Caine, I'm so glad you picked up the phone."

"Well of course, what if it was someone telling you that you've won the vampire lottery." He was chuckling a little under his breath.

"Well I have some interesting news, there is two young women following me home from the store. If you'd like to watch a little show please come out into the driveway." I said in a kind of sneaky voice.

"Sounds exciting."He said curiously.

"I'll see you in like 2 minutes." I hung up the phone.

I pulled into my well secluded drive way all the way to the end by my doors. Sure enough they were slow on pulling in, but they did come pull right in after me. They parked as far away from the house you could get without having to be on the gravel road. I grabbed the bags, they double bagged them I didn't ask them to, but they probably know that the bottles were heavy or something like that. I couldn't tell of course. Caine was standing outside smoking. He had no shirt on. His tan chest was just so immaculate. I just couldn't believe we have been worshiping each other in the sheets for the last week. I walked to him and passed off my shopping bags. I turned around and walked back to our little guest.

"Be nice." Caine whispered to me.

It was the two girls that were in the store and it looked to they were arguing. The tall girl was skinny. She was pretty in a mousy sort of a way. She wasn't the shade of green any more. But I just wanted to know what in the world she thought she was doing approaching a vampire at night and walking up her very dark drive way to meet her.

"Excuse me, hello. I'm Katie.You're a real live vampire aren't you?" Oh boy, this was going to be fun.

"No honey I'm a real dead vampire, but I guess it's all the same thing in your eyes." I said to Katie.

"Wow a real live vampire, you know you're the first one that me and my sisters ever seen." Katie said to, she said it like she was containing her excitement. Poor Katie excited to meet a vampire.

"Katie what's your sister name?" I asked.

"It's Jennifer." She said.

"Jennifer great."I repeated.

I walked up to her and started to guide her back to her car not quite touching her back. I just ushered her down to it, it reminded me of the way the sheep dogs drive in cattle except they nip them to get them to move. I leaned into the driver window and smiled a big smile full of fang. Her sister straightened up quick.

"Now Katie and Jennifer do I have your attention?" They both nodded in unison. I waved my hand. Just like a hello wave. It works every time.

"You'll get into the car and go home, where ever home is. Next time you see a vampire you won't be too eager to make friends with them. Now what are you ladies doing?" I exchange to her.

"We are on our way home." Back to the unison thing I thought it was adorable.

"What are you going to do if you meet another vampire?"

"Not be so curious." I couldn't have said it better myself.

"Well you two better get on your way."

Katie got into her car put it in reverse and drove away. I could have made it a horrible experience for her. Robbed her and told her all sorts of horrible things but I decided to let the two girls off with that mild warning. If they would have run into any other vampires they might have been good as dead.

I walked up and Caine, he was clapping a little bit with his full hands. I smiled and grabbed a bag.

"Your power is interesting, just a wave huh? I'm sure that can come in handy. Is that why you wear gloves?" he said it curiously, I smiled. I guess it was a better reaction than him totally freaking out and wanting to leave.

"Yes, I can also read people by touching them, find out what they are doing, done or if they're being honest." He looked curious again but didn't go into it that much.

"Like Dream Locking but you don't get into the trance like thing." He asked.

"Yeah-and I have to be out touching you and wanting to read you. I have to put a little concentration to it." I laughed a little. "So Caine please tell me what will your argument be for Tri Area South's King men ship?" I asked, since I curiously wanted to know. I didn't think it was done like it used to be, where the vampires who wanted the job all went after each other in an ultimate battle and last one standing was the king. Then again, how was I supposed to know? I haven't been to a leadership hearing in about a hundred years or so.

"I'm not worried about not being able to get rein. But if you'd earnestly liked to know I'll state that I have businesses here in the Tri Area also across the nation. I was thinking of purposing them with a queen." I looked at him and he lifted a brow to me. I never thought of being queen-ever. I guess Caine wasn't kidding when he said he was looking for companionship.

"Wow, maybe. I've never thought of being queen before." I stuttered that to him. I was a little shocked. Okay take that back a lot shocked.

"I hope queen is something you can get used to." He said it very persuasive to me and calmly. It made me want to giggle with excitement but I wasn't going to that be silly.

"What happens if someone else gets the rein?" I had to ask because I had to see if he was prepared for a lost as well.

"I'll have to let out the Dark Angel."

"Dark angel really Caine, you're going to go primeval on them?" He started laughing a slow light laugh. We sat down on the couch facing each other. He had a cigarette in his mouth and handed me the pack I got one too.

"The Archangel Michael came to me after I was cursed into Nod. He gave me a gift, or a curse-he touched me-that's when he declared me as an official watcher." He touched a spot on his upper chest that looked like a stab wound of some sort. I didn't pay any mind to it I thought he had it before he turned. "He made me the Angel of Darkness. He gave me this gift. I've tried to give it to other people before but I can't."

"So you've tried and you just can't; you're telling me that you can't perform the act of reenacting the gift?"

"They don't live through the process of receiving the gift." He said it like he was a little sad, but also like there really wasn't anything he could do about it.

I smiled to him. I was learning more and more about him. He was made into a dark angel of some sort by Michael the head angel in charge. He was also made a watcher so he had some anarchy in some sense to becoming godly. I looked on to him and he was right. He was a dark angel-he defiantly my dark angel. After this conversation I knew I had a lot to learn from Caine and realized he had a lot to teach me. I was excited to see where everything would lead. I was extremely intrigued and with everything blowing in the wind I was just going to let the chips lie where they fall.

CHAPTER 12

AFTER THE HOUSE WAS quiet I curled up around Caine on the couch. Some sort of fishing show was on the TV. I don't think we were paying attention to it. Every now and then Caine would turn to look at me, and we'd lock into each other's eyes. I was going in and out of his aura and the doorbell rang. I forgot I had invited my friend for company. He looked at me.

"It's Wendy and Ivan." I said.

He just sat up straight. I was glad we were both clothed. I walked to the door and open it. Wendy stood there vampire in hand-or maybe it was the other way around and Ivan had her in his hands. Hmm, it was really hard to say.

"Hello you two, Wendy-Ivan it's been a while since I've seen you how are you? Please come in." They walked in, Ivan more hesitant than Wendy. Wendy had been doing coke tonight I could feel the jones off her. She was looking to come down, or she'll go into the next day with no sleep. Not good I was thinking. It's not nice to know you have a drugged human running around your quarters when you're in your slumber.

"Cat, Yes this is Ivan you remember him. He came in just last month sometime." Ivan wasn't a very tall man, maybe 5'11; He had a dirty blonde hair and blue eyes. Thick lips and he had facial hair a light beard and mustache. When he smiled he was attractive in some sort of French boatmen way. I only remember him because Wendy had spent the week with him and it seemed like every time he was in town she'd disappear for a little bit. She got out her prescription to xanax's took four and swallowed with a forty of beer she had. Poor girl I was thinking.

"Ivan has some rolls if I'm not mistaking." Wendy said. I took a fake breath. It is a nervous twitch I have.

"Well before we get ahead of ourselves, this is Caine." Wendy's face changed to a confused look.

"No, I thought I had met your male companion. Dante wasn't it?" She stated. Caine stood up and came up next to me cigarette in his mouth.

"Among other things I'm called, Caine is my formal name. Wendy again a pleasure" quietly bowing but not taking his eyes off the human and vampire in the room. Ivan's eyes got wide after Caine introduced his self.

"You are Caine?" He stated to him. He just smiled.

"Yes I am Caine-Ivan Lucas I've watched you on television all the time it must feel good tricking those vampires in poker." Caine said. Ivan gave a smile. Vampires only played poker against each other. It was only fair.

"I enjoy playing poker. Well I enjoy winning at poker." Ivan said. We all started laughing after he said that. He pulled out a baggie from his pocket full of all different pills. He pulled out a smaller bag in the baggie and it had blue pills in it.

"They're called blue Hawaii, I don't know what is blue in Hawaii except the water and sky, but I don't get to see them blue so here goes nothing." Ivan said. Ivan spoke with a hint of a Louisiana boats men accent. He took two in his mouth and grabbed Wendy's 40 and took them with it, gave her two and gave me the baggie with the 4 left.

"Aren't we lucky love, we can experience blue Hawaii too." I relayed to Caine. Caine and I ran off to the kitchen, made some cocktails of vodka over ice I warmed up some blood. I brought out the cocktails. Wendy took a big huge sip of the cup I gave her and poured some of her soda in it and mixed it with her finger. That's my girl I was thinking.

Caine was very good at keeping company. He asked a lot of questions to Ivan. I think more so political crap than anything else. Have to get another vote for the rein I was thinking. But he seemed sincerely curious about the poker playing than anything else. I broke away and went to go sit outside, Wendy followed me.

"You guys are so cute!" Wendy whispered to me when I was out smoking in the backyard.

"Thanks, You thinking of getting series with Ivan?" she sat back and look at the stars lost in thought.

"I'm not sure. That wouldn't be so bad would it?" She asked me I just lightly shook my head no. "He has a steady work and he makes good money. I also love being with him-he treats me like a princess I'm lucky I found somebody like this." She whispered to me. I know that she spent the whole week with him the last time he was in town. He must go back and forth from where the tournaments are held at. I was genuinely happy for her I only hoped that Ivan would stay close and in this state so I wouldn't have to worry about her across the nation. He seemed well mannered enough to be a good companion. Well from the talking him and Caine did he seemed enamored with Caine. When we got inside Ivan came up to Wendy and rubbed his hand on her back sensually.

"I think we must go, I see this pretty little girl here and I'd like to take back to my house." He let the sentence trail off. He picked Wendy up and whirled her around. She was giggling like a school girl. It made me smile.

"Well that makes two of us." Caine looked at me and pulled me close to him.

I thought he was going to throw me over his shoulder and march me in the bed room. I looked at Wendy; she jumped on me and hugged me tight. She was fucked up and was always so funny and cute when she was like that. I was so glad she was done bugging out and was getting into the relaxed Wendy I knew. She whispered "Call me." Will do, I thought; I just nodded. They were gone.

I got up and collected the glasses that were left by my guest, it was only a little over 4:30am, they haven't been here but a few hours. Time has seemed to slow down to almost stopping since after I met Caine. I wonder if he had something to do with that.

"Why does everything seem like it is eternity with you. Time has stood still completely, I swear it." I said to him. I beamed a smile at him right after I said it. He came up fast on me and began to kiss me. I kissed back and he picked me up-he walked me all the way back to my room. He took my dress off and got right to work. I smiled to myself because this attention is was totally something I could get used to.

CHAPTER 13

CAINE AND I HAVE been inseparable. I have no objections. I know my body doesn't deny the fact that it loves what we do every day and every night. On a different note Dmitri wrote me an email. He told me he was thinking of me the day he wrote it. That's all he said. I think about him a lot. I didn't write him back, I have no clue what I'd say to him.

I went to work tonight-it seemed like any other week night to me. I do get werewolves in my club but they usually just come in pairs. They rarely ever come in by their selves and tonight I had a pleasant surprised with a whole lot of them. There were about ten sitting in my club when I got in today. I made my way to the back and change in my office. I was a little unhappy that I only had my 22 on me and there was so many in the club but I thought they must be celebrating something.

Mac Brien was the Biloxi pack leader. He had a big pack for the area with De Soto being so close. When I went out to the floor the half was getting dances and Mac beckoned to me. I approached and just hoped he'd be a gentleman because he usually annoyed me.

"Hey Mac what can I do you for?" I asked nicely because I didn't want to start the night in a bad mood.

"So I heard you had a new man Cat-some real ancient Vampire." I looked at him-I wanted to kill all the girls at my club at that moment because I'm sure it's by their mouths he'd know this-but

I just held together and smiled. I could sense Mac was on speed too. That only made me a little happy because they drink like fish while on it.

"You've heard right." I relayed to him.

"Yeah, word gets around. Especially since you have this joint, everybody wants to know what the Madam is doing with her strip club." He said swallowing hard on his beer who this 'everybody' was I'm sure it was the girls at my club.

"So Mac-what can I do you for?" I asked again-than Caine walked in. His eyes have never felt as strong as they did right at that moment. It almost felt like he was striking me dead with the look-huh maybe he was striking Mac dead? He was fixated on Mac-and his little posy. Caine stood up straight and I immediately thought there was going to be trouble.

My hostess brought Caine all the way back to the high roller tables. Everybody knew who was Caine was. There was no need to send girls to his table, and the girls wouldn't dare approach unless they had a death wish.

"Oh look boys. We have another in here tonight, what a lucky night for us." The bunch started to laugh.

"Not looking for any trouble here tonight. You are always welcome in the club, but not under any presumptions that you can cause trouble." He pushed the empty seat out from under the table and placed his feet across them. I gave him a look and he removed them just as fast.

"Don't use all those big words there, my crew won't know what you're talking about, and it's boring here in Biloxi, We can't pick on the tourist in the casino because we always get kicked out." Wow kicking them out sounded like a great idea but I didn't want any trouble from them, ever. And that would just cause more trouble, and come to think of it Mac Brien had a couple of small casinos he could go harass.

"Well Mac-If I can do anything for you just let me know okay. I'll be walking around so just get my attention."

"There is something I wanted to asked, Can Bruno here get a

stage dance for his birthday? I promised him a good time tonight."
He pointed to the huge one the really huge one. He made a gesture
like he wanted to whisper me a secret. I placed my ear close to
his face. "I promise his dad that I'd give him a night he'll never
forget." For Mac, that was a really nice gesture.

"Okay, that's a fine idea. I'll get that set up." I said.

"Thanks Catherine, You look awesomely fuckable tonight."
Mac said to me. I smiled a small smile to him. He could show a lot
more respect and still get respected as a pack leader I don't know
why he had to be a jack ass all the time. I squeezed his shoulder
with every ounce of my being not to crush it in my hand. He
straightened up when I reminded him not to fuck with me.

I nodded to Caine and took a stroll into the back. Wendy was
there chatting with Bailey. I didn't get her real name. Tony got
the ladies to fill out the applications. Wendy saw me, shot me a
brilliant smile. Did a striper run to me, which I am calling the run
you do in stiletto heels.

"Can you set up a stage dance for Bruno-that's one of Mac
Brien's pack? He's the really big one out there." She filled her
cheeks with air and popped them with her hands. "If I sense
you're on speed later I'm fining you 200 bucks. You know how
much I hate that shit!" I told her. She rolled her eyes and crossed
her heart.

Caine was looked extremely uneasy tonight. When I began
to approach him he never took his eyes off the wolves-not even to
look at me. I cleared my throat. He glanced at me.

"Werewolf's around you just makes me crazy. I don't like it."
This is the first time I've ever seen Caine not keep his cool. He
must have had a history with wolves.

"To relieve you they don't come in that much, and there isn't
much you can do about not liking it. This is a place of business
and my business happens to be a strip club." He looked at me and
poured me a glass of champagne. I took the glass and drank the
whole damn thing.

"I'll be right back; I'm going to talk to my staff outside." I said in a bitchy tone, Caine didn't seem to pay attention to me since he was so involved werewolf watching.

I was on my way to see Mike my valet. When I got outside I locked my eyes on him and started walking forward. When the other valets realized I wasn't out there to see him they all scattered.

"Mike, how are you tonight?" He was nervous, where does Tony find these people. Really he worked for me, he knew that, didn't he?

"Ms. Hope, yes how are you. I don't know what you've heard but I probably had nothing to do with it." Aw, he was worried that someone told on him, I wonder if he was giving my dancers a hard time.

"Mike I just wanted you to give me a 10pack. Here is 200bucks." He didn't take the money, he just went to a bag that looked like had trash of papers and he went to the bottom of it, pulled out a baggie. When he walked over to me he looked so nervous.

"I'm not fired am I?" He was worried about his job, good boy.

"Nah babe-and thanks honey." I winked at him and he seemed to ease up to a real smile. As I was walking back in I decided to scare my little valet boy into shape, with a blink of the eye I ended behind him, I had my hands on his arms by the shoulders and in a nice whisper by his ear I mustard out.

"My dear boy Mike, I just want you to watch out who you sell to and please not the girls before the shift, okay sweet heart." I said it in sweet tone, not using even a hint of glamour. He was nodding his head in a noticeable yes motion. Poor kid I was thinking. I walked back in and before I even made it to the door I heard the other valets walk up to him asking what it was all about. I'm going to have to spend more time outside with these parking boys.

When I got back in Caine was still staring at the werewolf's, but he had moved from watching the table to watching the stage. Bruno was on it right at the moment. He was cheering and raising his arms and he was being very animated about the stage dance.

There was even some other customers standing cheering. I made my way back to Caine.

"See Caine, they are just like regular men. They never give me problems and this is the first time this many of them came in usually it's just," He cut me off,

"Mac Brian." So he did know the pack leader.

"If you knew him and who he is why are you so aggravated at him and his friends right now?" I said in a very irritated voice.

"They can get out of line really fast. A lot faster than you could keep track of." He blurted out, very matter of fact like.

"Baby sitting a bunch of drunken werewolf's is a lot easier than babysitting a bunch of drunken vampires." I said back defensively. He fell quiet. I know he didn't feel he lost the argument but I think he was thinking letting me think I won it was a lot more rewarding than actually proving to me that I had my hands full. We sat and watched Mac Brien pack get many dances and they were spending fools for a good time. Watching the girls on stage reminded me of something Caine found in my house.

"I found something at my house that I think you'll enjoy. I set it all up and later I'll dance for you." I said to him in a very sensual tone. I will be honest with you I was a little excited I never dance. I play stripper by dressing up and it always surprises the customers when they get rowdy when my little ass is throwing them out of the club. They usually straighten up right away when they realize what I am-even though it usually takes until I show them my fangs they usually don't pick up on it right away.

His eyes met mine and seem interested. Then he leaned in and kissed me. I felt like I haven't been able to kiss him for the longest of times. I could feel Mac's eyes on me. After our kiss I looked and Mac was staring at me. He always stares at me. I never got that he's a werewolf and I'm a vampire we don't mesh. He's just like any other hot blooded man I guess.

It had only been since yesterday since I kissed Caine and it felt good to kiss him. It always my inner thighs throb. When locked into the sweet embrace the world could have stayed still and I wouldn't have cared. Caine waited in the club tonight after the club closed. After the regular night affairs that take place he walked me the car and told me that he'd follow me home.

I walked into the house and went through the kitchen door around the front towards the left. I was in there making cocktails and warming blood and I heard a bunch of commotion in the living room, a bunch of cursing I heard something slam into the wall, I rushed out there and I saw Caine pinning Dmitri against the wall.

"What the fuck is going on in here?" I said hasty like. I started to look around and there were candles and roses and rose pedals scattered all around. Wow, he snuck in to surprise me.

"Catherin what the hell is Dmitri from the Council doing in your house?" Caine said like he was out of breath. Dmitri looked at him, than me. His blue eyes piercing me so hard, he manages to get out.

"You're seeing Caine?" he was truly surprised. This was so not good. Doesn't anybody use the phone? What the hell was going on?

"Caine!" I yelled a little, "Having a Council member pinned against my wall will not score you any brownie points with them. Please let him go." After I said it he let him down. I was a little pissed off at Dmitri. He decided now to come over, now of all times.

"Dmitri, you really should have called."

"I wanted to surprise you." He said smiling at me. All I could think was yeah, I'm sure that it surprised you totally to get body slammed into my wall by another vampire. I started looking around noticeably.

"This is really sweet Dmitri, but you really should have called." I hated having to say that. He walked up to me and looked me right in the eyes. He didn't look hurt he looked more like 'Okay you can send him away any minute now.' Caine cleared his throat, Dmitri and I both looked at him.

"Do you want something to drink?"

I got a yes from both of them. Great I guess I'll have two guests tonight. Was I really going to turn away Dmitri after he went through all this setting up my house and taking the time out to surprise me with it? Huh-I knew the right thing to do and that was to turn Dmitri away. Caine and had plans tonight and the night was going to start running thin here in a little bit.

"After the blood Dmitri I'm going to ask you to leave. Caine and I had plans tonight. You really should have called." Caine was smiling a little I was glad my brown eyed beauty liked that. After the blood was done, Dmitri asked to say good bye to me outside. So I stood outside and said bye to him.

"I'll see you soon for the Council meeting, but if you want to come to Maryland before or after just let me know. I'd love for you to visit." Dmitri said.   He was being sweet. So I'm sure he meant it. I mean he wouldn't have gone through all this trouble tonight if he didn't, right?

"Okay, sounds like a lot of fun." I relayed to him.

When he was done telling me all the stuff we could do there. He leaned in and kissed me. I kissed him back. I like Dmitri. He gave my body what it needed and I wasn't going to deny that his actions tonight were appreciated. After the good byes I went back inside.

Caine didn't seem to mind too much now. He managed to find rolls in my purse that I had got from Mike and had a smoke waiting for me. He stuck a roll on his tongue and stuck that fat tongue in my mouth. I took the pill and swallowed I gave him a look. He went back into the bag and gave me another one. Good man.

I was so happy I had Caine's favorite suit on. I had my matching guns on still. My guns were so pretty I thought they were lined in ivory. My 19 11's are Liberty and Justice-if you think that's funny my 22's are called Humpty and Dumpty, I name my guns-do you got a problem with that?

I decided to continue as planned and I danced for my man. He loved it. Everything seemed to be going good, we were both naked again. I was sitting on my cat rug. And he came over to me and helped me up from the sitting position, he stood me up. He leaned into me and kissed me, like he'd never kissed me before ever, it was like he was trying to eat and in hale me. Then he leaned real close to my ear, and my vampire ears didn't fool me. He said sorry to me, all I could think is what is he sorry about?

CHAPTER 14

IN THAT MOMENT HE impaled me, his hand into my upper chest breaking my collar bone. Fingers conjoined like he was going to smack my heart, his thumbs pointed straight up, I screamed and started to try to get him to let me go, as I started to fight he stabbed his other hand into my other side of my chest with much more force than before that it went through. Right above where my heart is. I felt my shoulder blades break on the other side of me, it felt like my spine and ribs were being torn out of me. I was on fire. I wanted to die. I started wishing for death. I was bleeding out of my mouth so bad that I was swallowing blood. I was confused, so confused. Why was Caine trying to kill me? He picked me up off the ground hard with his hands still stuck in my chest. Was he praying? I was still bleeding from my mouth and my back bones were all still breaking and tearing. I hadn't notice but it Caine looked like he double in sized. He had a dark shadow behind him. But the pain grew, and then, and then it all subsided, than it was more action happening behind me than anything else. It was a constructing of my bones into a different form. I went for a breath knowing I didn't need one it felt good to do it. I breathed in and it felt like my back was stretching out. He released me and I fell to the floor.

As I was bracing myself with my hands, I was breathing more steadily and realized I was growing, I had grown different.What were these things I had grown out of my back? I stood up and looked in the mirror-the wounds in my chest were still there they just started healing now, but that wasn't what caught my eye. Caine was behind me and behind him were these huge wings, big bright beautiful wings. They enchanted me as I looked at them. Then I looked at my reflection and realized I had wings too. "Get the fuck out of here." I whispered that as it was stolen from my mouth as I spoke it, of course I didn't mean it literally, I was in shock.I looked at him I got scared and my wings kind of flapped a little. I turned around. I was just staring at him and his wings. I went to touch them and they started retracting. I could feel mine retracting.

I started to cry and before a second I was sobbing he carried me to the bed. He bit his wrist and gave me a silent order to drink. This was the first time I ever took blood from Caine. As old as he was, I just thought it might be forbidden. Being his companion or not, as I was drinking I could feel I was healing everywhere. It felt like my back and my ribs were all becoming normal again, but for some reason I was sure I'd never be a normal vampire ever again. I wasn't ready to ask why. I wasn't even ready to ask what the fuck he turned me into.

I was thinking how easy it was to persuade people into thinking he was the angel of darkness with the wings he had attached to his back. Why haven't I ever heard of the wings? I felt pathetic. What does that make me now? Could the wings fly me? Of course they could I thought. They are wings right. Caine placed his hand on my head.

"Let me tell you some things about myself. I lived as the Angel of Darkness for a long time. Centuries and centuries, I've tried to make another angel like myself. But all the times I had found someone who I thought I could give the gift to and they could be my companion they died. They died in the process of me making them into the angel." He was quiet. It seemed like he was thinking of what to say next."But you, you are my pure hope. You made me think I could try again." Caine said to me.

"So even though you knew other people died you still tried on me?" I said. I was hurt. Big time, I couldn't believe he could have been so careless with my life.

"I knew you were different. You are such an enigma. I don't think you'll ever know it. I knew when I felt you from Arkansas you were the one." What Arkansas? He felt me from where?

"What did you say?" I said like I didn't want to believe him.

"You don't do it all the time. When you get worried, but especially when you get lonely, you resonate an energy. It's beautiful. Please take this gift I gave you. I'll teach you everything. Be my companion." Caine pleaded to me. He just told me that my different moods send out a signal. What the flying fuck?

"Why hasn't a bunch of other vampires come to find me than?" I asked because I was a little confused.

"Vampires have to be older to appreciate the subtle energy you produce. Vampires now are not made the same blood. Their blood runs thin. Your blood is thick, it's thick like mine. I knew you were old. But when I found you and talk to you and met you and when I found out your name." He was high on something else. But he was saddened as well. "Please except my gift to you." He said.

I had to think. He did want a companionship. Even though this wasn't exactly what I was thinking it to be. In some perverse way I was intrigued, I wanted more of him. I wanted more secrets. I wanted to know everything. I didn't dare to stand up so instead I straighten up. Ran my fingers through my hair and placed it nicely on the front of me, covering my breast. I wanted to look presentable for my angel. He will be my king here soon. I am completely happy about that.

"Okay. I accept everything you'll give me." I said.

He leaned into me and kissed me. I felt so connected with him since I just took some of his blood. His sex was throbbing and sticking in my side I leaned over it and placed it in my mouth he moved some of my hair out of my face. I would go down slowly and suck on my way up under his protest noise he was moaning softly. He guided his self to lay flat on my bed and guided me to sit on him. I hovered for a second and sat on him my clitoris throbbed under the pressure of his cock. He was kissing onto my chest and he took his thumb to the knot in the middle of my legs. He was rubbing it vigorously. I was moaning loudly. He rolled over and thrusts wildly in and out of me. "Does it feel good my queen." He whispered to me. I looked at his face and he seemed to be so much at peace.

"Yes my king." He pushed harder into me. He ran his fingers through my hair thrusting his cock deep in my loins. My sex ached from the pleasure and became wetter and wetter. He growled a little and kept his speed. He kept driving his cock in me at the same speed and with a big breath out I felt my orgasm spread out of me. My sex was so wet he growled and with his own climax pushed deep into me. He shuttered on me after. He looked at my face and started to kiss me. I kissed him back. We lay connected for a brief moment. Than he rolled over and pulled me to be in his arms I guess now I was some sort of angel too. But what could this all mean? Only time would tell.

CHAPTER 15

I ENDED UP DRIVING TO Jackson. I wanted to take my truck since I had so much more room. Eagles were on, Hotel California. He was humming which was interesting to me, knowing he's heard the song more than the once to know the words. I guess he had all the time in the world to know every song ever known to man.

"So we'll check in, relax. The meeting doesn't start till tomorrow." Relax, I for sure needed it.

We past the convention center and I had notice they covered the wall of windows with dark fabric. It looked well did up for the convention to be held there. It was a big placc. I was excited to see about all that will get conducted here.

When we got to the hotel I handed the keys to the valet and he told them to get the bags out of the back. We walked into the Dae` Moon. It was humming with different vampires and their human servants. There were even some werewolves in there mixed in the crowd. You could smell them. I'm not a very big fan of weres` but I put up with them. Maybe I should be-friend Mac Brien. So I can have a little back up. Huh, I have Caine. But day back up would be nice.

"Hello welcome." The host shot a big smile full of braces to us. She was human I wonder how well she liked working for vampires? "Checking in? May I have the name please?" Caine was getting his wallet out of his pants.

"Caine Adamson." Wow, he had a last name. That is something I probably would have put together myself. I mean after all he is Adam's son. I was relieved it wasn't something completely hard to say or pronounce. Adamson was easy enough to say and remember. He looked at me. Gave me a wink and one of his sexy smiles, oh yum.

Once we were in the suite and I had my shoes off and I was unarmed I was in the mood for some kissing. I went in search of my vampire king. When we met each other's eyes he smiled and winked at me. I walked up and kissed him, opening his mouth with mine. When he stuck his tongue in me I bit him-he pulled back a little than locked in to a deeper kiss and started kissing me harder. We locked in our own world for a good little bit. When we were done with the heavy make out session we were in the bigger of the bed rooms of the suite lying on the bed.

For the first time of this trip I felt scared, not something I felt often. He was going to ask to become Royal of Tri Area South and he was going to propose me to be his queen. What in the world did that entail?

"So what is the case we will offer? I mean, I'm sure you have had time to practice your case while I was at work." I asked. He walked over to me. Took my hands, from what I could see he got lost in his own little world for a second.

"Like I've said I don't really think anyone will challenge me. I do have an idea for my argument. And if it doesn't work we will fight." I really didn't want to fight but since my little transformation I had become even stronger than I was before. I was a lot more in-tune with everything. I could hear the deepest darkest secrets in my girl's heads and even my partners head. It was a new outlook on everything. Besides the high that Caine's blood gave me. I broke about 10 martini glasses at work because I wasn't use to having all this new found strength. Every time I'd break one Tony would tell me go home that always made me laugh a little. Never in my wildest dreams would I have thought Caine would turn me into an angelic vampire. I would have never guessed he was an ancient angelic vampire. I always had a feeling the angelic vampire was the biggest oxymoron that I ever came encounter to.

"I guess I can call Wendy's cell phone. I think they are staying in this hotel as well. You never know they could be the other on this floor." He started unpacking but he did look up to acknowledge me. I started to get my phone from my purse; it was ringing when I started to retrieve it.

"Hello." I said.

"Hey Cat, when did you get into town? What floor are you on? We are on the 10th. You're at theDae` Moon right?" Wendy asked.

"We're on the 12th. So it doesn't look as we'll be neighbors but the same hotel is as good as it's going to get." She didn't seem to upset about not being total neighbors.

"There are four suites on this floor. How many are on your floor?" I only saw the two doors in the long hall.

"I guess it's only the two."

"What are you guys going to do tonight? The convention doors don't open till 6 tomorrow, well for the early risers." She was snickering a little. I was assuming that Ivan liked to sleep in.

"Caine said he has dinner reservations for us and he said he has somewhere else to take me afterwards." I started to laugh a little. "He even said he bought me a dress for the evening. I guess it has to be as he envisioned I guess." Wendy and I were laughing a little.

"That's cool, and after that? You could come here. Or we can go up to your room. What's your room number? Ours is 1004."

"We are in 1201 but I'll let you go for now. Call you when I figure we'll be in for the rest of the night." She hung up in a rush, I'm sure she was in the middle of doing something that consisted of having full concentration. Nothing came to mind what she could do that would need it or take it?

Caine pulled out a beautiful long white backless dress. It clipped around the neck and the clip was lined with gems. It had a deep v in it and it covered my breast area well it fit around my hip area and flowed down to the floor with a small train. It was extremely glamorous.

"Here love a gift for my queen." He handed me a white mink shawl. I was beautiful. And it was so soft.

He took me to a nice restaurant and we were enjoying our very old blood and a glass of extremely old wine year 1930, it was a very good year, we've talked about that before to each other. Then Vivian the Council member walked up, I did tell you that she was the president didn't I? Caine and I addressed her with a slight nod his more pronounced than mine.

"Hello, I'm glad to see you both made it Mr. Adamson and Ms. Hope, a couple for ages." I've said this before and I'll say it again, I don't care for this woman very much.

"I'm looking forward to your request on becoming the king of the Tri Area." She looked at me and raised her hand pointing at me a little "Bringing your lovely queen with you as well." She had herself a glass of blood than she smiled the most vindictive way "Things must be different here outside of your strip club, hmm?" As I went to answer back Caine grabbed my hand and gave it a tight squeezed.

"Vivian, I know you didn't come here to start problems. You'll hear are opening statements tomorrow. There's no need for this rudeness." Well I was glad that Caine was addressing she was being rude, I was just sorry he placed me in gloves. Vivian nodded as another vampire approached. I knew him, it was the other Council member, the vice president, and he also comes into my club all the time.

"You know Cal." She said to us. I nodded to him and looked right at Caine.

"You are hard to forget Catherin. I heard of you two were coupling now." Cal said. He had a genuine pleasant look on his face, for at least what I saw it to be. I smiled not one of my strongest suits as a vampire. I was nervously doing the breathing motions. Caine squeezed my side I guess to remind I didn't need to breathe.

"Well excuse us, it looks you two are trying to have a romantic evening, until tomorrow than." Vivian gave a slight wave. Yes I thought I'll wave at you tomorrow and really get you bitch.

After dinner the driver drove us down to East Amite Street there in Jackson. We pulled up to what looked like a church. Caine got out and told the driver to park and we'd be out a little while. He walked me to the door and opened it for me. It was late and I was surprised to see the doors open still. When we walked in he locked the doors behind us.

"I called and asked the father to leave the doors open for us." He walked me down to the front of the church. There was a huge crucifix at the end of the isle. I said huge right; it took up the whole end wall. He started to take his shirt off, and I started to stop him

"Really here? You want to be damned forever?" He let out a huge laugh and it made me feel so small and a little confused.

After he was out of his shirt he kneeled down and grabbed me and silently told me to kneel to. I did. He was breathing and that is not like him at all. I heard the rip and before I knew it his wings were out they were bigger than I remember them to be.

"Breath Catherin, I want you to think of the heavens. Think of the sky."He hushed his voice, "Think of me, think of you. Think of the stars and the moon." I closed my eyes, I didn't have to go into deep thought it was natural. My back felt like that ripping sensation. But there was no pain. I was steading my breathing and before I knew it we were both there, as god's anomaly-dark angels.

I heard a man speaking Spanish. He was walking out from a back hall. He was saying a prayer. He was the Priest of the church. He was in tears. Caine immediately started talking with him in a slow hushed Spanish. The Priest got on his knees and started prayer and crying harder.

"vienesparallevarme a casa." (you come to take me home)

Caine looked at me. I looked at the priest, I was wondering why he was thinking we were here to take him home.

"Me estoymuriendo de cáncer, y recé con tantafuerza." (I have cancer but I prayed) Caine looked at me and spoke in Greek.

"Πρέπει εμείς να τονξεκουράσει;?" (Should we lay him to rest?)

"τoaurthorities θα γνωρίζει από τα σημάδια δάγκωμα ότιήταν vamps." (they will know it was vampires.)

"Σας δαγκώματα θα πάει μακριάτώρα πουείστε ο άγγελος." (Your bites go away now that you're an angel.)I was overwhelmed. I mean do we really do this. Is this what we do?

"Catherin, we don't have to." Caine insisted to me.

"estoylistoahoraángelespor favor, llévame." The priest said. He wanted us to take him. Caine began taking my gloves off and I was just staring at the Priest.

"What do we do now?" I asked. I felt so foolish. Caine got a cup that I'm sure was used for the taking of the wine, or blood. And he bit his wrist and bled a little in the cup. Gave it to the priest almost like a communion way, the priest was hesitant at first but he took the blood into his self. Caine looked at me.

"Tell him that the angels came and told him that everyone must accept all gods' creators. Vampires werewolf's everything alike." Caine said to me. So I waved my bare hand to him and told him that we were god's messengers and told him the message Caine wanted me to say.

"Don't weep my love." Caine whispered and placed a finger to stop a tear from falling. We have to go. Caine's wings were retracted and mine were too by then. When we were leaving the priest yelled to us.

"no me va a llevar?" The priest whispered in a semi protest. Caine looked at me and smiled a little.

"Your cancer is gone now my friend. You are not ready to leave this world yet." The priest started crying again.

"graciasmuchas gracias" the priest said.

We turned around and we left. He walked us to the car gave the driver a wave and then waved him back into the car when he was getting out, I'm sure it was to open the doors for us, instead

Caine open my door, and I slid in, and he slid in behind me. We rode in silence to the hotel. When we got there, I was debating if I wanted to hang out with Wendy and Ivan or not. I felt we sure deserved it.

Every time tonight when I went to say something to Caine I got choked up. I didn't know where to start. This all seemed to crazy-even to me. Caine rubbed my back and leaned in slowly and kissed me softly. He got up and walked into the bedroom of the suite. I took a deep breath and came to the conclusion Caine would let me know what happened eventually.

"I just got off the phone with Ivan love.He and Wendy are on their way here." Caine said to me. That was totally unsuspected. He has been talking to Ivan so that means well they are becoming allies? This was sure news to me.

CHAPTER 16

THIS WAS NEWS TO me. Caine and Ivan were becoming allies. I shouldn't distress I don't think. I obviously don't know Ivan as much as I should. I was almost certain Caine didn't appreciate Wendy as much as I did. Did Caine appreciate Ivan in a different way-a way a woman may never know a man? That made me a little curious since Ivan seemed enamored with him when he met him asking him if he was Caine-like 'The Caine'. It's hard to believe sometimes.

"Caine have you ever loved a man like a woman?" I should have asked if he ever fucked a man but I know that would come off so classless.

"I havetaken a man to the bed. I know that's what you're asking me. But I prefer the woman's touch and fragrance, woman just smells sweeter than men do all around. There is no getting by it." He smelled my shoulder as he was saying it. I loved that he loved the way I smelled, your scent is your scent only, unless you have a twin, but your scent is your scent.

"So what have you and Ivan been up to without prying eyes of the woman in your lives?" Was that intrusive? Well you can't be classy all the time.

"Nothing like that my dear, I want to sponsor Ivan in his Poker tournament. I like that he has sass about sticking his nose up at older vampires." He said to me.

I regulated my breathing-deep breathe in deep breathe out.

There was a knock at the door so I jumped up to open it. Wendy practically jumped into my arms. She came in totting a small bag. I thought were they sleeping over. We did have the extra room. She finally got out that she knew we had an actual Jacuzzi on our balcony. Which we did I opened the doors earlier since I thought it was a bit odd to have doors leading outside on the 12 floor. Knowing Wendy she'd pick out the skimpiest bathing suit-but she'd probably just go nude because I would just go nude. So would Caine-I didn't know Ivan that well. But if he's like any other vampire he'd be completely alright with nudity. There really is nothing wrong with a naked body no matter what vessel it holds. I can only agree with that statement.

"Are you excited about tomorrow Cat?" Ivan asked me-he was being friendly.

"Honestly I have mixed emotions about it." I smiled a little to him.

"I don't think there is much to worry about. Caine has influenced a lot of vampires. I mean he is Caine." Ivan reminded me.

"Aren't you going to be queen or something Cat?" Wendy asked me.

"Well Caine is going to go for King of the Tri Area. He is going to propose a queen. We will just have to see how it goes." I said softly.

Before too long Wendy was filling the air with pointless chit chat and I couldn't help notice Ivan staring at me. He sat there glaring at me. He pulled out a pipe and took a deep hit. I lifted a brow to him what was this. Wendy was still on her little rant I wasn't even quite sure what she was even talking about now. Ivan walked to me and handed me the pipe I placed it in my mouth and he lit it for me. I took a deep hit-than I took another. I sat back into my chair and sank into a well-deserved drug induce semi dream. I needed this.

"I haven't chased the Dragon in forever!" I exhaled.

"Chasing the what?" Wendy uttered. Caine came to me and was rubbing on me, rubbing my head and my shoulders.

"I know you two just got here but help yourself to the Jacuzzi. I must take Catherin to the bedroom." Caine was smiling. I saw Wendy throw a semi fit from the corner of my eye-Ivan countered that by placing the pipe in her mouth. I guess there's a first time for everything.

Caine finally got me up and guided me back into the back bedroom where he started kissing me all over. I was still in a dazed. Well I'm calling it semi dream. When you're chasing the dragon you're not really awake, but you're not really sleeping. You're kind of a space out void of dream space. I wanted to know what the deal was. Caine locked the door behind us.

"It's just me and you, for a little bit, well until your high rests a little." He was lightly laughing. I started to kiss him, harder than he was kissing me. I was glad I change into sweatpants. I had my favorite Pink Floyd shirt on. It was a small so it really made my boobs look monstrous. He rubbed between my legs and I could feel the knot harden his sex was erect and ready to take lead. After we got through with our love session we lay in each other's arms.

"Stupid question?" Him with a stupid question, this is going to be good.

"Explain?" I said.

"Do you believe in love at first sight?" What an odd question, especially coming from him.

"Well I'm woman-of course I feel like love can be completed with one sight." He seemed happy with the answer. I got scared maybe he was telling me he found someone new.

"What if Ivan thought he finally seen Wendy with that glance, you know that look." So was he telling me that Ivan was in love with Wendy? That was great I thought. She'd be fucking thrilled. "Before you take it to a whole another level, he more so was thinking of turning her." If I had to breathe I would have been hyperventilating, I never thought of making Wendy a vampire. Okay, the thought had crossed my mind nearly a dozen times before, but this was for real doing it. Thinking and doing it is two different things.

"Has he asked her yet?" I asked. Caine was silent. I felt for long enough, so I made a small protest noise.

"Of course he has. She's well," I glared at him, "She was happy about the decision." I was a little hurt. Only because I felt I should have known more so than anybody else. Then again, I've never led her to believe that I ever wanted her to be turned. Have I not been that observant? Now all I could think of is when?

"When was any one going to tell me that they had talk to my best friend about becoming the undead?" I was throwing more of a fit more now than before; I was for sure really fucking agitated. Caine was following me around the room as I unpacked and threw things around. He stopped me.

"Ivan thinks its best you turn her. He doesn't want to be connected to her in a Master title." Go figure, I guess that was good for her. They still could love each other the same way. There would be no power struggle. He wouldn't be able to control her and her actions.She could still be her own person, well vampire I guess.

"I'll have to think about it. How fast does she want to end her life?" I asked. Caine looked thoughtful,

"She wants it for New Year's eve into the day. So the first day of next year she wants her new life to start." That sounded like my Wendy. I could always count on being dramatic. Wendy as a vampire, I hope she'd stay the talkative person she was now, thinking of that she'd probably talk faster and it would be hard for humans to understand her because she speed talked English. I wonder if she'd still want to work at the club. It would be nice if she did.

I'd have to talk to my friend tomorrow before we state our argument to the Council. I had no clue if anybody would go against Caine, but I'm sure there's some crazy old vampire that thinks they'll do a better job. Even though I wasn't so sure why we wanted to be in the lime light? I spent all my time trying not to be in that light, but whatever if Caine thinks it will be the best for us, I'm not one to judge him.I defiantly didn't know what the church thing was all about if Caine has all the answers he better start talking fast. I did trust him in some sort of odd way. He has shared so much with me already. And if he was a watcher who was he exactly watching all humans or all vampires? Caine thinks of a bigger picture that I obviously don't see. Like I said I trust him in some sort of odd way especially after my transformation. I really hope it wasn't all in vain.

CHAPTER 17

I GOT UP REALLY EARLY the next day, the sun was still up. To my surprise Caine was up and in the living area of the suite watching TV. I went out to the living area and strolled across the room, when he seen me he opened up the blanket to welcome me into it. I thought the blanket was a nice touch to him lounging on the couch. I got around the coffee table and slid in the space that was offered. I wasn't as scared as much as I was nervous. I wonder who'll challenge my king today. I wonder what they'll argue as there points. I was just hoping that they weren't too, how should I put this 'far the fuck out there.' Being vampires per se' well we really could lay on the drama thick.

"I got you a nice suit that matches mine. They're both an emerald green color. When I tried mine on I thought it would be perfect for you as well. Since both of us have dark hair and eyes. The shirt that I picked with the suit has a built in brassiere." Wow-he makes everything tickle when he tells me how he wants me to look. I leaned behind us and picked up the room phone. I called to the front desk.

"Hi Can I get 4 bottles of blood-2 O positive and 2 B positive. Also put me to room 1004." The lady on the other line was being annoyingly perky and then she placed my call. Wendy answered after the first ring.

"Hello can I help you?" Didn't she sound so professional?

"It's me. I was under the impression that Ivan likes his sleep?" I said.

"Yeah he does but I have to get up early to be ready in time for the meeting." She was doing something that didn't take too much attention at the moment though.

"So when were you going to tell me about New Year's?" I said. Wendy got quiet. Whatever she was doing she stopped completely.

"I was going to tell you when the time was right. When Ivan and I were going to announce that we were going to be together." She uttered like a child getting caught doing something she wasn't supposed to be doing.

"My answer is yes, I will." I could feel the smile beam at me through the phone. She started shrieking in giddiness.

"Oh my god Catherin, you don't know what this means to me, us. I am so happy. You know you doing it would make it so we could never be apart as well. Isn't it exciting? Ivan is going to be thrilled thank you-thank you!" I was glad to have gotten such a great reaction. Even Caine was smiling behind my head.

"I'm going to let you go. I guess we'll meet in the lobby at quarter to 8." She was agreeing with me and said she'd be there earlier than the time I stated. Which was completely fine with me? We said our good byes and I turned around to hang up the phone. Caine started smelling my hair.

"That was very sweet of you." I liked that he thought so. "You've probably made her year." I was thinking she wouldn't think so. She'd probably think her year maker was when Ivan said he wanted her to be his permanent partner.

I wonder how having Wendy as a child would be. I've known her long enough to feel like a mother. Placing a caring hand on her shoulder and telling her to sleep it off. Or maybe it was when I would break up fights with her and the other girls at the club and them realizing I was her friend more so there's.

We showered together and got ready to go. At least we tried to shower together it wasn't working very well-being naked around each other always seems to head us towards a different directions of things. I put on a little make up. Even though Caine says I don't need any-I loved playing dress up. The suit looked fantastic. I didn't think he knew my size since it change so much on what clothes I wore, which made me feel so wonderful. I know that he has had many hours to study my body and he knew it very well. It was just amazing feat for any being.

We walked to the elevator from the middle of our hall. While we were waiting two human women walked out from the other room. They were painted up really whore like, but they both looked like more expensive whores than anything else. I notice one had bite marks on her neck. Their heads were buzzing on something, an older wine, and bourbon.

"Hold the elevator!" the taller of the two yelled. That would be a great feat I was thinking since the elevator hasn't gotten to our floor yet. They walked to us and they were smiling a lot. Mostly at Caine, the shorter of the two, the one with the marks on her neck started a rant of some sort.

"I just love these things. We come all the time. There is supposed to be some ancient vampires stating a claim into royalty tonight. It's going to be exciting." I looked at Caine, he winked at me. I started smiling. The taller one leaned into me, she had been drinking. She smelled of old booze.

"You look so familiar. Where have I seen you before?" I just bowed my head a little, keeping my eyes on both of them. When the elevator door open the bell hop bowed, "Ground floor?" Caine and I both nodded the yes motion.

"We're getting off on the 6floor, honey!" The shorter of the two bellowed. When we stopped on their floor the short one leaned into Caine and whispered; "If you're looking for a good time it's room 634." She winked at him.

"The whisper wasn't necessary my dear woman, my partner could hear you just fine. Now I'll have to convince her not to pay a visit to you." He smiled and he had his fangs out. She straighten up looked at me and marched her ass right out of the door. I just thought booze really was liquid courage, or liquid stupidity. The bell hop closed the door out of no were the bell hop started with his own little rant.

"They are here during any vampire event. The hang out at the lobby bar, they're really pathetic if you ask me." In a weird gesture I started thinking he was defending me and my honor. The bell hop cleared his throat, "Ground floor." We gathered into each other's arms and walked out toward the front of the lobby.

When I saw Wendy she was stunning. She had half her red hair up in aloose bun. She had a white fur shall, it was made of fox. Real too-so I must have been a present from Ivan. Her dress was spaghetti straps, the part that covered her breast were shaped into triangles. Her dress was a deep purple color. She looked great. She even had some contacts on, Blue. I thought that Ivan should tread lightly so she didn't run off with anyone else, but for as long as I've known her she has never been that kind of girl. Good girl for her.

I guess Ivan Lucas was a pretty straight 'A' vampire. Him not going off to make Wendy a vampire and wanting me to turn her more so than him I never claimed Wendy as mine. I don't feed off her so there was no connection there except her actually being a friend of mine. I did know Ivan brought humans and vampires alike to my club. He contributed to the money I made and I will say that was very well appreciated.

We were picked up in a limo. It was nice, white. I thought it was excessive but you know we like excess. It makes it easy being what we were. At least we didn't walked out and fly there. Wendy would have had to have caught a ride with Ivan but it was easy to fly with someone.

When we got to the convention center we walked in to a woman vampire sitting at a table, she was talking to another vampire, and I knew this vampire. He was a count prince. I met him many centuries back in, where was that, Romania. He looked as handsome as he did when I first laid eyes on him. He was giving orders to the vampire sitting at the table. I'm glad that the name tags were stickers and weren't any pins to ruin our suits and such. He smelled me because he whipped around and glared right at me. His eyes widen as he approached so casually fast that if I wasn't with another vampire I might have thought he were about to get attack me.

He looked at Caine and in a sign of respect removed his hat and bowed his head a little as he asked for my hand. I was so glad I did slip on the lace gloves Caine had gotten me with my suit. I placed my black laced hand is his hand and he kissing my hand in a weird sort of gesture. I am vampire, I don't get embarrassed but the way he was acting was making me very uncomfortable.

"Relax my dear prince. It's great to see you as well. I still have to sign in and report." He smiled and placed his top hat back on his head.

"My dear Catherin, it's a pleasure to see you again, I heard you were coming to this event." He was doing a slight bow and he was being extremely charming. Just a hint of his Hungarian accent peeked through. "Your gentlemen Caine is acting so polite, but he'd like nothing more than ripping me limb to limb and giving my dead again carcass to the wolves in the room." I gave a slight smile because I never thought of Caine as being the jealous type. But the Count was an older gentleman vampire as well so maybe he knew something I didn't.

"We will catch up later. I have to get back to my party, they are waiting for me." I said softly to him. He just kept the same smile on his face.

"Of course, I will talk to you after you and your partner have made your cases. I'm part of the vampire Council you know?" I didn't know that. So they traveled far, and they got around. I gave a slight nod and released his hand and hurried back to Caine.

For the Council there were 12 but I only seen the 5 on the list, I suppose you can't have everyone here, it would make for some vampire activists to come with their fire bombs. There was Vivian the president, it had Cal as vice so I mean that's good. Dmitri we know him, Raymond, he resided here in Mississippi. He was the governor forTri Area south, he'd probably still stay here and help govern the area after they pick a king. Then there was the Counted Prince Vladimir.

After we walked in we had a little area waiting for us near Councils table. I saw Ivan had a seat right in our section, if that was Caine doing who knew. They were closing the door for the trial to start. Or whatever you wanted to call it. Dmitri seen me and bowed his head, gave me a slight smile. I did the same. It seemed out of nowhere this small red man jumped up and started boisterously speaking to everyone in the room. He was about 5'2, had white blonde hair. He was a reddish color which made me wonder if he actually a vampire at all, I only could tell by how unbelievably loud he was.

"Of course we know all about the brother killer in the mist, and his whore of a strip club owner." Wow, I beg his pardon, I know that vampires are one's to be ruthless but that was just plain classless.

"That's Guy." Ivan whispered to Caine and I. "He's a boatman in Louisiana and has a few ferry boats there for the tourist. He's a big time gambler, and he feels like she should have rein here in Tri Area. He's been here for over 90 years easy." Caine leaned back a little.

"I've been here longer." I was looking right at this short little red man and immediately didn't like him.

"If it is true than Caine here is all of our makers. We know of the stories don't we. I say there are all lies. Lies made by the ultimate con man that's old and likes to use our romantic nature to win us over. He gets us to follow him. He gets you to listen to his stories, to believe his lies. Then he destroys them saying they've broken every rule that he has ever laid down." He paused for a second.

"Are you donc with you speech?" Vivian asked.

"Not yet. He brings us a woman less of a punishment as her ancestor. But with all sense in place is still a whore where she stands. You can't think of letting a woman who is an owner of a strip club be your queen. Her ancestor was gods punishment to man." He paused for a second. "She even named her establishment Pandora's Box." Gasp and whispers broke through the crowd. I mean are these vampires for real.

Caine started clapping. That was it. I thought Caine has gone completely mad. Caine jumped on the table and started with his speech.

"Does everyone feel the same way as Guy here? If so why hasn't anybody tried to assassinate me? Maybe it's the whole thing of killing the divine maker and we all die. Let's test out that theory shall we, any takers?" Everybody fell quiet. No one moved.

"I own a lot of business in Tri Area south. In all three states also across the country, I've been here for more than a century. I have been through it all. We would be the best choice, Catherin has been here for a small eternity herself and besides her night life affair business she is an avid member of the Council and pays her dues when owed am I right Vivian, Cal? I am the beginning but Catherin's blood runs as thick as mine, she's is one of the oldest vampire I've ever came across besides myself. I would never pick someone that I didn't think could handle being queen to defend her area."

Vivian stood up and Cal lifted his hand and Vivian sat right back down. Cal got up and everybody in the crowd started to whisper again.

"I think all of you should place your votes for Caine. I know we in the Council will. He by far is our entire senior. He is after all the beginning." Well it was good to see Cal believed the stories.Guy grunted and started to speak, Cal lifted his hand and Guy stopped speaking. "I've heard enough from you today. You're completely pathetic." If anything were to destroy a vampire Cal's statement made him slump into his seat like he just been hit with an invisible hand. It made me think what exactly Cal had really to do with the Council.

After a few hours it seemed that everybody was being as normal as they could be, at least for a bunch of vampires. Vampire's stopping by telling us congratulations, I was wondering how much time was going to go into being the king and if it takes too much time up if I'd end up alone again. Dmitri didn't come to say anything to me. He seemed busy with everybody else there. There were many woman vampires that wanted his attention I observed. I wasn't sure if I was jealous I sure was amused by the vision.

Guy seemed to avoid us like we were the plague. I thought that was the best thing for him to do. He really was a miserable little man. He surrounded himself with many men of all walks of life. They were all per se' 'Pretty boys'.

There wasn't much more to say. We had another day at the Council meeting. Caine was collecting numbers I stayed chatting up with Ivan and Wendy. It's nice to stay with people you knew. I was getting to know Ivan more. I like what I seen. I wonder how much traveling entails with him and his poker tournaments. If he was going to make Wendy his partner I'm sure he's prepared to take her with him. That was always a plus. I wanted nothing but the best for her. After all she is my friend, all right best friend and you don't come by many.

This day was interestingly over. And it didn't go anything like I planned. I was just happy we didn't have to fight. That was a plus. But there was always tomorrow. I guess we will have to see how it goes.

CHAPTER 18

"You look beautiful. Is the dress new?" Caine beamed it at me.

"No-it's not. I've had it for some time now. Do you really like it?" I asked. I loved this dress. I just wanted to soak up all the complements I could get from it. It was a plan dress, but it was in scarlet red. It was loose in the front and covered my breast loosely, tied into a nice tie at the top and hung on my body. It was a silk material. It was beautiful. I had got it on sale, just cause you're a vampire doesn't mean you can't get a good deal.

He walked up to me and kissed me running his fingers through my hair. I was glad I decided just to put thick big curls into it. No up do tonight. It was the second day of the Council meeting. This is when they say who won the rein. After Cal's little rant I did some snooping. From the rumors Cal is Vivian's maker. He was there when the first Council came to. Like our friend the count he's Hungarian. He's name real name is Vance. Vance morphed into Cal, sometime in the early 1600's. He seen the beginning of the Council and he has always been there to enforce the rules and way things are to be. The reason why Vance-or Cal was so good for the Council, his power is to sense if you're lying or not. I can tell if I touch you, it's impressive to just listen to someone talk and know if they are telling the truth.

We got into our limo it was black tonight. I don't really care for blacklimos. Wendy and Ivan were sitting closer to the driver in the middle of the limo, and we were sitting by the doors. We were about a few miles away from the convention center when a huge semi-truck slammed into us from the left side pushing us onto the right side. This was no accident. There was another car right after that slammed into the back of the limo.

Wendy screamed. The driver was hurt bad he was bleeding profusely out of his mouth. Since the limo was on its side. We needed to get out through the sum roof but it was stuck.

"Break out the window" I yelled to Caine. He slammed his closed fist into it. He put a hole right through it, than he worked out the safety glass.

"Ladies first, Wendy come here." I yelled to her. She was next to me balancing awkwardly in the sideways vehicle, as soon as I thought we were in the clear. Boom! Someone threw a bomb and the car was on fire. The only thing I could think of was we must have pissed these people off. The only person that came to my mind was Guy. I started wrapping Wendy's coat around her face and helped her out of the car. Caine took out the back window and Ivan and he were getting out through the back.

Once I was out, I tried to get out the driver. But the fire was going really good. We needed to save the driver we couldn't let him just die. God I didn't want to think of the press. Caine had his jacket over his head and he went to the driver's side and started slapping the flames. He got to the door and ripped it completely off the hinges, he manage to get the driver out and we went to the side of the road. I could hear the police coming. I was dirty covered in black smudges of dirt, soot, and I had glass pieces everywhere in me. I was feeling pretty lousy, Caine was pissed. You could feel his anger roll off him like the way the fire rolled off the car into waves. I didn't even know what he was going to do.

"So does this mean we are still going to the meeting?" I asked I guess I was in denial to some sense.

"Yes we are, and we are going to see what Guy has to say about this." Caine growled under a breath.

"I'm coming too, that guy ruined my dress." Wendy said. I

always liked this woman. Ivan walked up and kissed her on the forehead. I guess he really did care for her. Well as much as a vampire can care for someone.

After talking to the police, getting the driver in the ambulance and Wendy getting some air from the ambulance we were free to go. But we didn't have a ride. The police didn't want to give us a ride because someone just tried to kill us and they didn't want to get caught in a civil fight amongst vampires over any type of leadership struggle. Ivan grabbed Wendy gave us a silent nod and bam, he was in the air. Well we weren't that far so flying would be the best thing to do I guess. So I went to take the air. And realize I couldn't.

"Caine I can't fly." I said. He leaned into me.

"Sure you can love." I mean was he telling me to sprout my wings and give it a flap.

He walked into the shadows he took his shirt off and he was in his wings. I guess I got lucky with my choice of dress since it was backless. I walked into the dark and got into them to and he held my hand and we were airborne. Wow this was exhilarating and extremely fast. We landed. It took me a second to figure out how to, first time flying with the wings.

I had about it to my neck with surprises for the night though. Some of my hair was burned my clothes were covered in black smudges. My finger nails were dirty. I smelled like smoke. Right at that moment I just wanted to find Guy and kill him. I don't even want to know why he wanted to kill us.

We burst into the party. We got a lot of gasps and shocked faces. We walked toward the Councils table. In an instant Dmitri was by my side.

"Catherin, what happened? Are you all right?" Dmitri seemed really busy with everything that was going on, beside yesterday where he just stared at me during the meeting and argument. I'm sure he was shocked himself when Caine offered the position of queen to me. It was comforting to know that he still was concerned about me enough to leave his table position to come to sooth me.

"I'm fine, someone ambushed us. Try to kill us." I said to him. Dmitri looked pissed he started to scan the crowd, if I wasn't mistaking he was growling. Caine was standing next to him and they met each other eyes. For the two men in my life they seemed to get along fairly well. I mean after that incident at my house, they didn't try to kill each other after the fact.

I saw Guy and jumped up and toward him. He seen me coming and countered and used my weight against me and slammed me into the wall. I should have seen that coming. It wasn't in vain. Caine had Guy from behind and had his arms pinned behind his back. He wiggled but there was no getting Caine to release his grip. Dmitri was making a clear path towards the Council table. Vance and Vivian looked up. Vladimir stood up.

"What is all this about?" Vivian stood up and exclaimed.

"Guy tried to kill us, Cal please asked him." I relayed to them. I wonder if calling him Vance would be too much.

"Is that true Guy?" Cal asked. He was leaning back in his chair. I like how this vampire felt he could be so nonchalant with everything.

"I'll never say!" Guy grunted under his breath.

"You will say." Cal spoke it so loud and with so muchauthority I shuttered a little. Guy started to cry. He was mumbling something.

"Speak clearly." Cal ordered.

"I wanted the rein. I don't believe the stories of Caine. I wanted to show ever body that he could die and that we would still be here dammed into this world. How can you let his whore," Dmitri was squeezing his throat now.

"Witness here today all Tri Area South members-avid Council followers this is a crime by great offense. The punishment is death. By law of Caine, Catherin if you'd do the deed, I'm sure you have a gun somewhere on your person." He was waving his hand like he had already exhausted himself.

I had to smile somewhat to myself. I did have my gun around my thigh and I was extremely happy I brought my 19 11's. I also was extremely gracious that it didn't come off in the crash or in flight, silver bullets of course. I got the gun out, and people gasp, really why is that shocking people still. I walked up to him took the safety off.

"Hold him out a little Caine." As he held him away from his body I took aim and fired 3 rounds into his skull. After that Caine dropped him to the floor. I took my gun and fired two in his chest. Caine dropped him on the floor the puddle of blood started to work out around him. I was glad Caine brought his coat and shirt with him even though he was standing there shirtless I went into his coat and got myself a cigarette lit it with my zippo and dropped the lit zippo on Guy's dead again body. He caught fire quickly and just like that-his after life was over.

2 Weeks Later

"Wendy you'll be a beautiful vampire." I was comforting my Wendy who was being unreasonable about looking absolutely perfect for her day.

"That's what Ivan said." She half smiled. I really was thinking how many times she needs to hear it to believe it. But that's my Wendy.

It was late and I was ready to go home. We had stayed late because Wendy wanted to talk in private since the clan was going to be in tonight. It was nice that Caine could pull himself away from his work to hang out for the night.

He managed to take rein near the coast and he runs everything through his home. He said if I wanted to I could stay by his side while he was awake but lately I've been spending all my time at the club. I get him at least once or twice a week' that was good enough for me.

Things have been going good. Dmitri called me and invited me to Tri Area East. I accepted his offer. I had been dreaming of him lately. I'm pretty excited, and I leave on Monday....

CATHERIN HOPE'S 'V' CHRONICLES
VOLUME 2
SNORT & KILL

CHAPTER 1

BALTIMORE IS A CRAZY town. Downtown is always busy. So I've been told. I see there is tons of traffic. Dmitri picked me up from Dulles International. My flight was on time-11:17 on the dot when I landed. He was there with 24 long stem roses in a bouquet. He was such a gentlemen or a ladies` man. I had to ask to make sure he didn't have a change of heart on me. He still claimed he wasn't the gentlemen I claimed him out to be. I was thinking it was all a façade he wanted to play. So be it-I won't push. We drove back to his place with mild chit chat. How's the weather down south. How's business running Blah-blah etc.-etc.? He lived in a penthouse right in the downtown area. His home was a warehouse converted into apartment complexes. I could tell by the freight elevators we used. It was good to know that no one would come to bother us due to the key he needed to push his floor.

I have to say it myself Dmitri did very well for his self. His condo or apartment was probably double the size of my house. It had many rooms. I could tell from all the doors that I saw. He offered me the other half of his apartment for my stay but I relayed to him I'd get lonely. It seemed to please him a great deal that I was saying I didn't want to be alone.

When you exited his elevators you were met by two towering windows. They took up the wall in front of the elevators. You could have either gone left or right. We went towards the right. When you entered the right side you came to a mini hall. I notice his wood floor. They were a deep mahogany color. It was really nice, also a big plus on my side since I hate carpet. After the hall you got into to a huge kitchen. I wonder if he bought this place from someone who actually ate food. The fridge was massive. The size would hold many bottles of all sorts of things. I'm sure if he wanted to he could entertain guest easily. The kitchen had a dining room attached and it open up to a fabulous sized living area. The living room had a huge flat screen TV mounted on the wall. No cords so he had it done professionally. He also had a nice sized stereo system hooked up, no cords for that either. Passed the TV on the left was a hall. There were windows lined all the way down the left side of his apartment. The hall had many doors in it. I wasn't so sure what he'd needed all the rooms for. I wasn't one to ask so I guess I'll never know. All the rooms looked like they wouldn't have windows in them, so I guess that was a plus.

Dmitri rushed my bags down the hall. All the way down the last door that was facing the living room. It's like my house because my door to my room did the same thing. I'm almost certain that he whisked my bags to his bed room. He walked back to me looking flushed in the face. Was he blushing?

He looked so devilishly sexy. I remembered why I liked him so much. He looked like a bad boy that made you feel like a good time-all the time. He strutted towards me like he was listening to some silent music I couldn't hear. He took something out of his pocket and placed it in his mouth. When he got to me he leaned over me which was easy for him to do and kiss me. He pushed what he put in his mouth in my mouth and it was an ecstasy pill-so much for the Council having higher standards then us regular vampires. I kissed him back after I swallowed it. With a lot more force than he kissed me with. After a good minute he stopped me, can you believe that-he stopped me. Ha, it made me want to laugh.

"Before we get that started I have somewhere to take us." Okay that's a good excuse, I guess.

"Really-so late?" I had to wonder it was later into the night. I did jump an hour ahead. Well it was well after midnight. But I guess we would still have many hours of darkness. Maybe I was just a little annoyed because I was impatient for Dmitri's love. Well body, ok he's great in the sack.

"Do you not like surprise's" He asked back to me. I didn't have to think about that at all. I hated surprises. I gave him a thin eye and he started laugh. I was glad he was finding it so funny-since I wasn't finding it funny not one little bit.

"You look fabulous. Do you travel this sexy all the time?" I started to wonder why he'd ask me such a thing since Caine picked out the suit I was wearing. It was Navy color skirt suit set. I was wearing a fitted red top that almost look like a corset with a bra on top. It laced in the back, but it was just for show because it zipped up on the side. The skirt was a little on the short side. I was packing so I wouldn't walk around without my jacket either. I wonder if Caine knew Dmitri would have liked my suit as much as he did. I know those two had a history but I guess I have to wait to find out-I know when time is right they'll let me know.

Dmitri in the car was telling me that he never gets to drive in his city. Also that he feels so privilege to be driving around with someone as stunning as me. He looked well driving. I told him he emanated a sexiness that you couldn't deny while in the driver's seat, it made him swerve. That was all for show-we are vampires we would never swerve. I did make me smile though, and I don't mind one bit to smile at Dmitri.

We pulled up to a regular building. It almost looked to be an office building. I was a little confused and out of nowhere though a man in a cream suit opened my door. There was a man on Dmitri side of the car in the same cream suit. On the right breast plate was the initial DP. I gave him an eye after they opened my door. He gave me one back and place on that same old sexy smile. I exited the car and waited for a second. Dmitri got to me and placed me into his arms. We walked into these unusually large doors and at the end of this short hall was an elevator. When we got onto the elevator the bell hop had a cream suit on too. It had the same initials as the valet. The bell hop asked "All the way up?" Dmitri looked at him and repeated the words.

"All the way up." We did go up, all the way up.

When the door opened it was pretty much a room full of drunken vampires, well mostly drunk vampires, there were drunken humans in the room too. I suppose if I were a human I'd have to be drunk in a room full of vampires too. After taking a breath, I started to regret the roll I dropped in Dmitri's apartment before we left. I swear I got introduced to about 100 different people. They all knew who I was and were addressing me as your highness. All that crap made me want to gag. I guess in these moments though I can understand why Caine wanted me to look so presentable. We walked straight to the back and up these stairs about 20 maybe more-I don't have OCD that bad where I count them or anything. The office was nice, it was enclosed in glass. It over looked the magnificent dance floor. It had two red leather sofa's facing each other and in the middle of the couches was a black coffee table. I could feel the bass from the club and I could make out some words of the song playing. I was starting to feel that the office wasn't very private but as soon as the thought crossed my mind Dmitri locked his office and the glass fogged up. Wow that was spectacular. There were two pieces of glass that didn't fog up. They were high on the wall you could only really see the ceiling from them. I guess if the vamps really wanted to they could jump or fly to take a peek in here.

Dmitri got a phone call almost immediately after we entered the office. I didn't know how long he'd be so I decided to get comfortable. I took my jacket off. I was armed but Dmitri didn't seem to mind. I walked over to him and started to unbutton his shirt. He told who ever that was on the phone that he'd call them back. I was thinking to myself-good call. I pulled out his ponytail so his hair could hang on his shoulders, there was no protest. He grabbed a little around my waist then stuck his hand up my skirt, he place a big smile on his face and put his head on my lap. He whispered the words "No" I just started smiling. I knew I wasn't wearing anything under my skirt he obviously didn't. I started to undo his pants and pulled them down to let his man hood show. He helped by raising his bottom to help me with the process. He was erect I guess he was extremely happy that I was making these advances to him. We stared into each other's eyes for a brief moment. I love looking into Dmitri's eyes. After I felt it was enough I leaned in and started to kiss him. His tongue slipped inside my mouth in and out at rapid speed. He was eager like always. Well technically I was more eager the first meeting with him than him but that was after the fact. I ran my fingers through his hair. I tasted blood which was fine with me since both our fangs were out. If I bit him-if he bit me, well we can't be certain who did the deed. After the fact it was a nice touch to the kiss. Dmitri still had his hand up my skirt. He was unbelievable with his fingers pushing on the little knot in-between my legs and penetrating me at the same time. He pushed my skirt to my waist and guided me to the front of him. Than he guided each of my legs to each side of the chair and he slid me down into his lap inserted his sex into my sex. My leg shivered and I let out a moan, it was pure ecstasy. Besides the ecstasy I was on, it was 10 folded the feeling I was feeling. With each stroke digging deeper and deeper in me the heat that he was causing me a tingling sensation through my whole body. We were kissing very intensely than someone knocked very loudly on the door. I jumped up on the desk and had my guns pointed at the door.

"There better be a fucking riot outside." Dmitri yelled to the door.

"Sorry sir. There is a gentlemen here requesting you presence. I told him you were indisposed but he won't have it any other way. He needs your presence and he said to bring the queen as well." That made me curious. Dmitri gave me an eye as well.

"Tell him we will be right there." Dmitri said still very annoyed.

"Right sir I'll let him know right away."

Well I wasn't going to leave Dmitri like this. I put up my guns and he gave me a half smile. It looked like he was starting to pull up his pants so I got to him fast and stopped him. I winked and he smiled. I got onto my knees and placed him into my mouth. I did slow and steady movements, but I didn't have to do too much he was erect and throbbing before even a small fraction of a moment. Before I knew it half of his things on his desk were on the floor and we were rolling with each other. He was being more aggressive now thrusting into my sex with a lot more force. It sent chills throughout my body.

"I'm going to cum Cat climax with me." He said while in my ear. He started to rub the knot in between my legs and I started to get hot and it was a rush. I don't know if it was the ecstasy but whatever it was a rush. I was happy that the club was so loud since we were extremely loud for are climax. "You bring something out of me." He said to me laughing a little.

"Now what would that be Dmitri?" I asked smiling.

"I looked forward for your visit for some time now so we could perform these acts again. I don't usually feel like this about anyone." He was looking at me right in my eyes.

I placed my jacket on and he gathered me into his hands and unlocked the door. I immediately looked to the bar area, to see if I recognized the gentlemen waiting. I didn't so it made me wonder all thatmuch more peculiar on who this man was. I was leaning on Dmitri because my roll was full blast by now. I was tingling all over the place and I felt like rubbing everything that moved. This really wasn't the best way to meet someone for the first time. I hope I can control myself on not wanting to rub my hands all over his body. It made me want to laugh so badly. I leaned into Dmitri's ear.

"Let's make this quick so we can go back to your place and be alone." He smiled, his smile was even sexier now that I was feeling the way I did. We walked up to the man in waiting. We got a noticeable head nod from him.

"Good evening." The man eagerly said to us. "Thank you for meeting me on such short notice. I hope I didn't interrupt anything." I looked at him because he probably could smell that he interrupted something. "I'm Vegas." He got out after pretty quick. He was a younger vampire maybe 20 years in his afterlife. He had a cop feel so I was almost certain he worked for the Baltimore PD. He had short blonde hair cut like he was in the military. Well I won't stereo type it but it wore his hair really short on his head. He had brown eyes. They were kind of a hazel color. He had a thick chin with a dimple in it. His blonde mustache seemed to complete the look. He made me feel uncomfortably almost immediately and I wasn't so sure why.

"Hello. I'm Dmitri Holiday the owner of the Drop Pitt. This is Catherin Hope queen of Tri Area South. You came to see us, so please speak your mind we were on our way out." Oh goody I thought he's whisking me away.

"Yes of course. I'm tracking Trevor Belmont. I've come to the understanding that Ms. Hope here has had connections to him before in the past." He said.

"That's true, but I haven't talked to him in over a century." I relayed that to him. I was lying threw my teeth. I just seen him maybe 20 or 30 years prior to this conversation. "What kind of trouble has he got his self into?" I only asked because I had been slacking on my job. Honestly speaking I haven't started tracking any one on the bounty list at all. Dmitri gave me a suspicious eye like you bad girl.

"It seems he goes to a party and at the end the vampires end up going on a slaughtering spree killing humans and vampires alike." Wow-that was pretty big. It almost sobered me up. "An incident happened here so it's imperative that I speak to him." He said. He seemed excited like a little puppy.

"Well like I said I haven't heard from him in a long time, but since he's here in the States now you can be certain that he will track me down soon enough. When that happens I'll turn him over to the Council and I will for sure call you too. I promise we will get to the bottom of all this madness." I relayed it to him. Vegas looked back and forth from Dmitri and mine faces. We both had blank looks on them.

"Well if he happens to get a hold of you, or you just mysteriously end up talking to him here's my card. I would appreciate a phone call. We have a lot of questions for him." I looked at his card and it said Detective Vegas. Huh, funny-he is a cop.

"Well if that's all we will be on our way." Dmitri relayed him. We all exchange head nods and Dmitri was whisking me off to the elevators. The drive back to his apartment felt like the longest ride. But when we were in the elevator we weregoing at it kissing and rubbing. From the elevator he picked me up and carried me the full length of the apartment. He brought me through the door at the end of the hall and I saw my bags by the door. This was Dmitri's bedroom and it was huge. He actually took my skirt off and tossed it and he was a little confused by the top so I unzipped it on the side. I tried not to rip his clothes off and I think he was trying not to do the same thing. He laid me on the bed every so softly and we actually had soft passionate love all night long. The sun wasnipping at us when we finally were finished with the night escapades. We drank from each other and I was drunk of his love and his blood. Made me wonder why Caine didn't take blood from me. With my first night done I was happy I said yes on visiting him. It had been a long time waiting.